STAR TREK
PRODIGY™

A DANGEROUS
TRADE

STAR TREK

PRODIGY™

A DANGEROUS TRADE

Written by Cassandra Rose Clarke

Based on the television series created
by Kevin & Dan Hageman

Based on *Star Trek* created by Gene Roddenberry

Simon Spotlight
New York London Toronto Sydney New Delhi

SIMON SPOTLIGHT
An imprint of Simon & Schuster Children's Publishing Division
1230 Avenue of the Americas, New York, New York 10020
This Simon Spotlight paperback edition January 2023
TM & © 2023 CBS Studios Inc. Star Trek and all related marks and logos are trademarks of CBS Studios Inc. All Rights Reserved. Nickelodeon and all related marks and logos are trademarks of Viacom International Inc.
All rights reserved, including the right of reproduction in whole or in part in any form.
SIMON SPOTLIGHT and colophon are registered trademarks of Simon & Schuster, Inc.
For information about special discounts for bulk purchases, please contact Simon & Schuster Special Sales at 1-866-506-1949 or business@simonandschuster.com.
Cover art by Alecia Doyley
Book designed by Kayla Wasil
The text of this book was set in Basic Sans Alt.
Manufactured in the United States of America 1222 OFF
2 4 6 8 10 9 7 5 3 1
ISBN 978-1-6659-2118-3 (hc)
ISBN 978-1-6659-2117-6 (pbk)

CHAPTER ONE

Jankom Pog pulled back the cover of the *Protostar*'s transporter console—and immediately let out a long groan of dismay.

"This doesn't look good!" he said, whipping out the scanning feature on his multi-mitt, which took the place of his right hand. "Jankom Pog will be very upset if he gets turned into a targ when he's transporting."

"Jankom? What's wrong?" Gwyndala looked up from her maintenance work to find Jankom frowning down at a panel set in the ship's wall. They were in the transporter room, where the ship's computer could send them down to nearby planets, or even to another ship, on a beam of energy. Assuming they were near any planets or other ships, which at the moment, they weren't.

"One of the phase coils!" Jankom's multi-mitt whirred as he shone a high-powered light on the panel. "It's all worn down." He looked up at Gwyn and gave her a toothy grin. "You don't want to see a transporter malfunction."

"I'm sure I don't." Gwyn set aside her own work and went to stand beside Jankom. While she had some idea of the technology that went into the transporter system on the *Protostar*, she was no engineer, not the way Jankom was, and to her the phase coils looked the same: as shiny and bright as everything else on the ship. "Are you sure it's worn down?"

"Pos-i-tive!" Jankom attacked one of the coils with his multi-mitt, loosening it up so he could show Gwyn the imperfections that he saw. "Look here. Smooth as the bottom on a Melvaran mud flea." Then he popped the coil back into place and turned to Gwyn. "It needs to be replaced."

"Replaced?" Gwyn's eyes went wide as she considered all their options. "I guess we'll have to power up the replicators, then."

"Ah, no can do." Jankom shook his head.

"Replicators can't handle these bad boys." He slapped the phase coil, and it rattled around in its panel. Gwyn felt herself cringe.

"Um, should you—"

"Jankom Pog knows what's too much!" He laughed and smacked it again. "But it will need to be replaced soon. Otherwise, you might wind up with your foot growing out of your head next time we transport you!"

"Wait, you mean we can't use the transporter at all?" Gwyn looked up at the transporter pads in horror.

"Oh, Jankom Pog thinks we can get three or four more transports out of the coil. But then it's blitz-o!" He chuckled.

Before Gwyn could respond, a familiar face—and equally familiar shock of gray and white hair—popped into the transport room. Dal R'El strolled in with a cool air, making a show of examining the space. Gwyn resisted the urge to roll her eyes.

"I thought you were monitoring our flight trajectory," Gwyn said.

"I was," Dal replied as he plopped down in the transporter station chair. "But then I remembered

I needed to check on my favorite engineer."

"Well, you've got great timing," Gwyn said with a smile. "Because Jankom found a problem."

Dal's only reaction, however, was to give an easy grin and straighten his spine. He ran a hand through his hair. "The captain's ready to hear it."

Jankom immediately began laying out the problem of the transporter phase coil.

"So we replicate it," Dal said.

"Too late," Gwyn said. "I already suggested that."

"The replicator can't solve all our problems!" Jankom let out a loud, exasperated sigh. "Jankom Pog has spent a lot of time studying this transporter. Look." He popped the phase coil out of place again and held it up to the light. "See those squiggles there? In the metal? Those have to be programmed by hand. Replicator can't do it." He put the phase coil back and slid the cover in place.

"So what are you saying?" Dal asked. "What are we going to do? We're going to need to use the transporter eventually!"

Jankom crossed his arms over his chest and looked at Dal straight on. "We need to buy a new phase coil."

"Buy?" Gwyn blinked. "With what currency?"

"Yeah," said Dal. "We lost all our chimerium, remember?" He threw his hands up in the air as he slumped back dramatically in his chair. "We're broke!"

Gwyn looked over at Jankom, who shrugged.

"We should call in the others," she said. "Maybe Janeway knows of a secret stash of chimerium on the ship?"

"Doubtful," Dal muttered, but he still tapped on his combadge. "Crew, this is your captain speaking. I need everyone to meet me in the transporter room. We've got a problem." Then he dropped his hand into his lap and beamed triumphantly at Gwyn.

"You didn't have to make it sound quite so dramatic, you know."

"Our transporter is busted!" Dal said. "I'd say that's an emergency."

"Not busted," Jankom interjected. "We just need to buy a new part."

"But we don't have any way to do that," Dal said. "Which is why—"

Voices echoed down the corridor: the bright, cheerful chatter of Rok-Tahk and the calm, soothing lilt of Zero. A second later, Rok-Tahk burst in through the doorway, Murf cradled in her arms.

"What'd you bring him for?" Dal asked.

"You said everyone!" Rok-Tahk responded, and Murf cooed and rubbed his head against her chest. She giggled.

"And you said there was a problem." Zero drifted in after Rok-Tahk. Where Rok-Tahk was strong and solid, her body like carved granite, Zero was light and compact, their true form contained in a makeshift containment suit. "It sounded serious, in fact."

"You forgot to call Janeway," Gwyn said, before raising her voice slightly and speaking to the ship. "Janeway! We might need your help."

Instantly, a human woman materialized next to the chair where Dal was still sitting. It was Janeway, the ship's holographic training adviser.

"Help?" Janeway raised an eyebrow. "And here I thought the six of you had the running of the ship down."

Dal rolled his eyes. "Well, we ran into a problem."

"Just tell us what it is!" Rok-Tahk cried. Murf wriggled out of her arms and made his way around the perimeter of the room, investigating the equipment.

"Don't let him eat anything," Dal said. "Otherwise we're going to need to dig up even more chimerium."

"Chimerium!" Janeway cried. "What do you need chimerium for?"

"Jankom, tell 'em."

Dal sighed, and Jankom launched once again into the issue of the transporter's worn-down phase coil.

"That does sound like quite the pickle," Janeway said when he was done.

"Agreed." Dal sat up, shaking back his hair. "We were hoping you'd know where there's a secret stash of chimerium on the ship."

Janeway laughed. "I'm afraid there's no such thing. As crew, it'll be your job to find a workable solution."

Dal groaned, throwing his back against the chair. "Greeeeeeeeat," he said. "What are we going to do?"

The crew exchanged glances with one another, concern flickering across their features.

"Maybe we could ask someone for it," Rok-Tahk said. "Like, another ship? Maybe they'd let us borrow one of their coils."

Jankom laughed. "They'll need it for their own transporter!"

"But what if they have a spare?"

"It's possible, but unlikely," Janeway said. "And this far into the Delta Quadrant, we don't tend to run across other ships that frequently either."

"Janeway has a point." Dal rubbed his chin, considering their options. "But we can get to a market easily enough. We just need money." He frowned, settling deeper into his thoughts. The woman who raised him, a Ferengi named Nandi, had taught him all about the importance of money. Of course, that had led to her selling him to the Diviner, who forced him to work in the Tars Lamora mines, so maybe her perspectives weren't entirely trustworthy. He certainly wasn't going to sell any of his crew—to the Diviner or anyone else—just to replace a phase coil. But if they had something else—

Dal snapped his fingers and sat up in his chair. "I've got it!"

"You do?" Gwyn smiled a little. "This should be good."

Dal lifted his chin. "We'll use the vehicle replicator."

Jankom threw up his hands. "Jankom Pog already told you—"

Dal grinned. "Not to replicate the phase coil. We replicate something else, something people will pay chimerium for. Then we use the money to buy our new phase coil. We can go to a market on a nearby planet. Or we find someone willing to trade, which would be even easier!"

He beamed at the crew. Only Janeway didn't look excited.

"Ooh, that's a good idea!" Rok-Tahk said. "What could we replicate, though? Won't most planets have their own replicators?"

"Not Federation-quality replicators," Gwyn said excitedly. "And the vehicle replicator makes parts that non-Federation planets probably haven't ever seen before."

"Yeah!" Dal cried. "Like a ground vehicle battery, maybe?"

"Do you think that would fetch enough for a new phase coil?" Gwyn asked. "Jankom?"

"Jankom thinks so!" He clapped his hands together. "In fact, Jankom can go fire up the replicator right now—"

"Wait." Zero drifted forward, their portal swirling with light. "This doesn't feel quite right to me, I'm afraid."

Jankom sighed. "Aww, c'mon, Zero. You're no fun."

"Zero's right." For the first time since Dal had declared his grand idea, Janeway spoke up. "Dal, what you're proposing doesn't fit in with Starfleet protocol."

"So?" Dal said. "We need the phase coil. We're going to have to use the transporter eventually."

"Surely it's okay to break protocol sometimes," Gwyn added. "When it's absolutely necessary?" Her gaze darkened. "I broke protocol when I helped all of you escape from my father."

She didn't have to add that her father was the Diviner, the very same man who had imprisoned Dal and all the rest of the *Protostar* crew.

"Yes, but that was the morally right thing to do," Zero said.

"Replicating a battery to sell isn't exactly immoral," Dal argued.

Janeway's frown deepened. "Yes, I think this goes beyond a question of protocol," she said.

"Zero raises a relevant point—that this might not be the most ethical use of Starfleet resources."

"What's so unethical about it?" Dal shrugged. "We're not doing anything to hurt anyone. In fact, we're helping someone—we're giving them access to a battery they wouldn't have had otherwise."

"I suppose you have a point," Zero said.

"Besides," Dal continued. "We're not doing this to make a profit, the way the Ferengi do. We'll sell the battery for the exact amount we need to buy a new phase coil."

"That seems fair to me," Rok-Tahk said. "What do you think, Murf?"

Murf looked up with a gurgle. He was currently in the middle of swallowing the other transport station chair.

"Murf only cares if he gets to eat at the market or not." Gwyn smiled.

"Well, I think that decides it, then." Dal stood up. "Jankom, let's head down to the vehicle replicator."

"Are you certain?" Janeway quirked an eyebrow. "As captain, it falls on you to ensure your crew is meeting ethical standards and practices."

"We all agree," Dal said. "Don't we?"

He turned to the others, who all nodded. Murf burped. The chair was gone.

"We need it for the ship," Rok-Tahk said. "Remember when Dal used the transporter to give back the crystal that Nandi stole?"

The crew nodded. It hadn't happened that long ago: Dal's old caretaker Nandi had talked them into taking a remalite from a nearby planet, but the life-forms who lived on the planet needed that crystal in order to communicate. Fortunately, Dal had been able to use the *Protostar*'s transporter to beam the remalite back to its rightful owner.

"Couldn't have done that if the phase coil was busted." Dal grinned.

Janeway looked at each member of the crew. "If that's what you think is best," she said. She sighed, and a second later a coffee mug materialized in her hand. As she took a long sip, she said, "I suppose there are worse ways to use a vehicle replicator."

CHAPTER TWO

*C*reating the ground vehicle battery only took a few minutes, the vehicle replicator humming and glowing as it built the battery out of thin air—or rather, energy, as Jankom had explained to the rest of the crew. Replicators used energy to create almost anything, from clothes to food to ground vehicle batteries.

"That was the easy part," Dal said. "Now we've got to find someplace to sell the thing!"

He and Jankom packed the battery in a simple, nondescript case and carried it to the bridge, where the rest of the crew was crowded around the starmap, a massive hologram that showed a cross section of the charted star systems of the Delta Quadrant.

"What have you found?" Dal asked. "Anything standing out to you?"

Gwyn frowned at the starmap for a moment. "There are a couple of possibilities." She tapped the starmap and the image zoomed in on a small moon orbiting around a gas giant. "First up is Tai'shyi." She tapped on the moon and information flowered out in the air of the bridge, detailing the planet's population, climate, and major cities. "There are a bunch of small communities here that might be interested in purchasing the battery."

Dal squinted as he read the key information about the moon. "It says here that Tai'shyi has two Federation colonies," he said. "I'm not sure that's the best place to take a replicated Federation vehicle battery."

Gwyn frowned, the light from the holo illuminating her skin. "You might actually have a point there."

"Yeah, course I do." Dal grinned. "What else have you got?"

Gwyn sighed and tapped her PADD—a personal access display device. The holo swooped around to show another planet, a dusty swirl of green and gold with a few narrow veins of dark blue. "Here's Odaru," she said. "No Federation ties, but there is a sizable Ferengi and Orion population."

Dal chuckled. "So lots of people looking to make a deal, then."

Gwyn nodded, smiling mischievously as she tapped on her PADD. Locations on the hologram of Odaru blossomed with pinpoints of light. "In fact, there are several markets on the planet, none of them with a particularly stellar reputation."

"Perfect," Dal said. "The last thing we want is people asking too many questions about where we got the battery."

At this point, Dal and Gwyn's conversation had captured the attention of Zero, who was still wary about the entire enterprise. The crew had already found themselves in some tough situations, and Zero knew better than the others how cruel the sort of people with not-particularly-stellar reputations could be.

"What exactly do the ship's records say about the markets on Odaru?" Zero asked, drifting closer to the hologram. They lifted their visor to the informational output, reading silently to themselves. It was just like Gwyn had said—a high population of Ferengi and

Orions, two civilizations that Zero knew were more concerned with profit than safety. It made sense that they'd both have populations stationed far out in the Delta Quadrant, away from the watchful eyes of the Federation.

"They say that this place is perfect for us," Dal said confidently, crossing his arms over his chest. "That they're full of the kind of people who won't ask questions—"

"They also say that there's a high level of criminal activity!" Zero cried. "Look at those statistics! Armed robbery? *Murder?* We—"

"Will be fiiiiiine," Dal said with a grin. "Don't worry. I've run deals in places like Odaru before."

"Really?" Gwyn peered up at Dal, an amused expression on her face. "And how well did they work out for you?"

"Got me and Nandi almost fifty bars of chimerium," Dal said proudly, sitting back down in the captain's chair. "Without anybody getting murdered. This should be a breeze."

Zero still wasn't entirely convinced, but as they looked around the bridge, they had the sense that none of the others shared their reservations. So they didn't say anything more.

Dal spun around in his chair, pointing one finger at the viewscreen of the ship. "It's decided," he exclaimed. "Set a course for Odaru!"

It didn't take long for the *Protostar* to reach Odaru, and when Dal asked Rok-Tahk to drop the ship out of warp speed, the planet gleamed in the viewscreen, its greens and golds and blues even more vivid in real life than they were on the map.

Dal let out a long whistle. "Look at that," he said. "Too bad we don't have much time to explore, huh?"

Gwyn glanced over at him. "The last few times we went exploring strange planets," she said, "things didn't exactly go smoothly. Remember that planet that tried to eat us?"

Dal waved his hand—Gwyn wasn't *wrong*, exactly. The planet had indeed tried to eat them. It had also made them hallucinate. And it almost destroyed the *Protostar*.

But still. That didn't make the idea of going down to the surface of Odaru and seeing what those swirls of color looked like up close any less appealing.

"Jankom!" Dal called. "Do you have the battery?"

Jankom responded by lifting the case where he and Dal had placed the battery.

"Perfect."

"How are you planning to get down to the surface?" Zero asked. They were drifting near the ship's controls, having helped Rok-Tahk navigate the *Protostar* to Odaru. "Jankom said we only have a handful of uses left in the transporter. That limits how many of us we can send down."

"Good point." Dal leaned forward—he'd been so caught up in getting down to the market and getting his crew the phase coil they needed that one logistical detail had slipped his mind. "Jankom? What do you say? Should we risk it?"

"No way, no how." Jankom shook his head. "Better to save the uses we do have."

"Yeah, I was thinking the same thing." Dal nodded at Zero. "Let's land the *Protostar* on the surface."

Zero turned around in their spot and fixed their glowing, multicolored gaze on Dal. "Are you sure? We've already seen how desirable the *Protostar* is to ... to those with less scrupulous morals."

"You think someone down there would want to steal the ship?" Dal asked.

Everyone looked over at him, the expressions clear that they did, in fact, think that. Even Murf burped out an agreement.

"Okay, that's fair," Dal said. "Not going to argue at all. Who wants to stay behind to keep an eye on things? Zero?"

Zero made a soft, disapproving noise. "I don't think that would be the best idea," they said softly. "I don't know if I can fully protect the ship."

"Of course you can," Gwyn said. "We all trust you!"

Zero hesitated for a moment. "It's not a matter of trust," they finally said. "But I'm noncorporeal. Without a body, how well can I fight, if things come to that?"

"I can stay," Rok-Tahk said brightly. "As long as someone stays with me."

Murf slid over to her and looked over at Dal, his eyes hopeful. But Dal shook his head.

"I think we're going to need you," he said to Rok-Tahk. "Someone's got to carry the battery through the market."

Rok-Tahk frowned. "Can't Jankom do that?"

"Yeah, but you—" Dal jumped up from his chair and strode across the bridge in a few easy steps so that he was standing beside her. He tilted his gaze up until they were looking each other in the eye. "You'd be even more intimidating than Jankom!"

"Hey!" Jankom said. "Jankom Pog is plenty intimidating!" To prove his point, he stomped around the bridge, punching the air. His demonstration was brought to a quick end, though, when the case containing the battery swung up and hit him on the side of the head.

"Yeah," Dal said slowly. "I think Rok-Tahk will be better. What do you say? Designated battery holder?" He nudged her, and Rok-Tahk let out a defeated sigh.

"You still haven't decided who's staying behind." Gwyn stepped up to Dal and Rok-Tahk, her arms crossed. "If Zero goes down, that leaves just me and Jankom to stay behind. And you'll need Jankom." She smiled. "He's the one who knows what part we have to get."

"Exactly!" Jankom added.

"So you'll stay?" Dal asked.

"That wasn't what I was offering!" Gwyn sighed. "Zero, are you sure you don't feel comfortable staying behind?"

"I'm sorry," Zero said. "But you're the much stronger fighter—"

"Zero has a point," Dal said. "And, Gwyn, you're the only one of us who *really* has a weapon."

Gwyn sighed, her hand going to the heirloom bracelet she wore on her wrist. It wasn't just a bracelet—with just one thought, she could make it any shape she wanted. Including all sorts of weapons.

"Fine," Gwyn said, even though she really did want to go to the market too. A thieves' market? She couldn't even begin to imagine all the things she could experience there. "But Murf is staying with me."

Murf gurgled happily.

"Works for me," Dal said. "Janeway!"

The hologram materialized in the middle of the group, a bemused smile on her face.

"Janeway, we've decided to land the *Protostar* on Odaru's surface," Gwyn said. She scowled a little. "Murf and I'll be staying behind to keep an eye on things. Do you think you can help us?"

"Of course," Janeway said, her eyes sparkling.

"Deciding not to use the transporter, I assume?"

"Yep." Gwyn smiled.

"A good call."

Their roles decided, Dal asked Zero and Rok-Tahk to bring the ship down into Odaru's orbit. "As close to the biggest of the markets as you can possibly get," he added. "Which is—"

He whipped his head over to Gwyn, who had already pulled up the holomap. "Orgora Market," she said. "In the southern hemisphere. I'll send you the coordinates."

"Received," Zero said, and the *Protostar* began its descent into the atmosphere, oxygen burning up brightly around them as they dropped lower and lower, eventually breaking free to the view of a vast swath of emerald forest intersected by lines of dark blue: the rivers that crisscrossed the planet. As they approached, a city appeared up ahead, glittering in the sun.

"I'll bring us down into the forest," Zero said as the ship moved closer toward the trees. "That should give us some cover."

They guided the ship down toward the largest of the rivers cutting through the woods, then followed its path. Zero dropped the ship low, skimming along the water's surface. Light danced across the viewscreen: sunlight reflecting off the metal of the ship's body.

"Wow!" Rok-Tahk said, her eyes as big as saucers.

"It's not bad," Dal said, although secretly, he agreed with her.

"Coming to a landing now," Zero said as the *Protostar* slowed until it was hovering just above the river. Then it began its diagonal turn, and Zero nestled it among the huge, towering trees, tucking it away out of sight.

"Great flying," Jankom said, slapping Zero on their metal hull. Zero rattled in response.

"Why, thank you," they said demurely.

"Yeah, not a scratch on her. Jankom Pog can tell." Jankom nodded his approval, then turned to Dal and Rok-Tahk. "You ready to get us that phase coil?"

CHAPTER THREE

*T*he *Protostar*'s ground vehicle bounced through the narrow paths among Odaru's magnificent trees, the low-hanging branches slapping against the vehicle's shields and making them buzz and light up. Dal clung to the dash, and Jankom took a particularly sharp turn to avoid running into a thick tangle of tree roots sprouting out of the ground.

"Why did I let you drive again?" Dal wailed as he was tossed sideways up against the door.

"Because Jankom Pog replicated this baby!" Jankom jerked hard on the controls, and the vehicle spun to the left, barely missing another outcropping of smooth, arching roots.

"Slow down!" cried Rok-Tahk from the rear of the vehicle. "Zero almost flew out the window!"

"I'm fine," Zero said—although they didn't exactly *sound* fine. Dal twisted around to find Zero clinging to the rear window. Rok-Tahk clutched the carrier containing the battery to her chest as if it might keep her from being flung out of her seat.

"You okay back there?" Dal asked with a smirk.

"Watch out!" Jankom sang out.

Before anyone could respond, the vehicle launched into the air. For a moment, there was a sense of calm, as if they were floating in zero gravity. Zero loosened their grip on the door. Rok-Tahk let out a sigh.

And Dal turned back to the front, expecting the worst, and finding it.

"Jankom!" he shrieked, because the vehicle was heading straight for the trunk of a tree as thick around as the *Protostar*'s warp drive. The smooth, reddish bark filled Dal's vision, and he braced himself against his seat. "Turn! Turn!"

"Jankom Pog is turning! But the tree came out of nowhere!"

"Are we going to die?" Rok-Tahk said in a tiny voice.

"No!" Dal shouted, not knowing if it was true or not.

Jankom gave a tug on the controls, and the vehicle jerked sideways and clipped the tree with a shatter of bark and energy-shield flares.

"Found the road," Jankom said cheerfully.

He had found the road—and the vehicle was about to crash-land onto it.

In the backseat, Rok-Tahk and Zero both let out screams of terror. Dal told himself to stay calm, as difficult as it was with the narrow road barreling straight toward them.

"Wait!" Jankom yelled. "The antigravity!" And then he slammed his multi-mitt onto the holographic controls.

Immediately, their free fall halted, and the vehicle, along with the crew tucked inside, drifted down to the road with the grace of a feather caught on a breeze. They landed without so much as a *clank*.

"Told you Jankom Pog had this," he said with a grin as the vehicle switched modes and sped down the road.

Dal slumped backward, his heart racing. "Maybe fewer theatrics once we get to the market."

"Yeah!" Rok-Tahk stuck her face into the front seat. "You almost killed us."

"Jankom Pog was in control the whole time," he said, patting the vehicle's dash.

Rok-Tahk sighed and settled back into her seat. She turned to Zero. "Are you okay?"

"Y-yes." Zero's voice had a slight waver to it. "Now that we're on the road."

"Yeah. Me too." Rok-Tahk looked down at the case holding the vehicle battery. Now that they weren't crashing through the forest, she felt a new fear coiling up inside her. She still wasn't totally sure about going into Orgora Market as the designated battery holder. What if someone tried to steal it? What if she had to fight them to get it back?

She curled her big fingers around the case—it looked so small in her hands. But just because she was big didn't mean she liked fighting.

Jankom zipped the vehicle down the road. It wasn't long before there were other vehicles on the road too: mostly small, personal vehicles, narrow little things that held only one or two people. They flashed by, engines whining.

"Joyriders," Dal said. "People race them and stuff. Or just ride them for fun."

"Seems like it would be easier to just use a transporter," Zero said.

"Maybe not everyone here has a transporter," Rok-Tahk said.

Suddenly, their ground vehicle shot out of the shade of the forest and into the glare of Odaru's brilliant, stone-white sun. Straight ahead, the city glittered like a diamond.

"Are we really going there?" Rok-Tahk gasped.

Jankom pulled up the holographic map, their vehicle a small blue dot blinking its way across the terrain. "Hmm, not exactly. Looks like Orgora Market is on the outskirts of the city."

"Makes sense. Most thieves' markets are," Dal said confidently. "If Orgora Market is anything like the Endan Bazaar on Arp, half the stalls will be legit, and the criminals will be all mixed in. If they get word that the authorities are coming, they'll scatter like that." He snapped his fingers. "At the Endan Bazaar, they had this whole underground tunnel system set up so people could get away." He grinned, twisting around to look at Rok-Tahk and Zero, who were both gaping at him. "I might have been down there once or twice."

"Fascinating," Zero said, just as Rok-Tahk said, "You did not!"

"I did." Dal winked.

"Well, then, maybe you should be the battery holder." Rok-Tahk shoved the case at him. "Since you're the one with all the experience."

"No way!" Dal said. "I'm the one that's going to negotiate for us. It's better if I have my hands free for that."

"What does that have to do with anything?" Rok-Tahk said.

"Just trust me," Dal said gravely. "I—"

"Wow!" Jankom interrupted. "Look at that!"

Rok-Tahk and Dal immediately quit their argument to turn their gaze to the massive sign glowing over the road. ORGORA MARKET was emblazoned in flashing neon in at least twelve different languages—Dal recognized Ferengi and Federation Standard, which Janeway spoke. Arrows blinked in the direction of a turnoff in the road, and as they gaped out the window, the crew caught their first sight of the market.

"Are you sure that's not the city?" Rok-Tahk gasped.

It certainly *looked* like a city. Buildings were clustered tightly together, and small personal vehicles like the joyriders they'd passed on the road zipped in and out of them. Signs glowed in the air, advertising Klingon food and Orion trinkets and ship parts and treasures from the Alpha Quadrant. Jankom slowed the vehicle and pulled it over to a designated parking area, where people from all different planets clumped together, clutching their purchases.

"Wow, this place is huge!" Dal cried, because it was easily the biggest marketplace he'd ever seen. But when he realized how awed he sounded, he straightened up, coughing into his hands. "I mean, we should be able to find a phase coil easily."

"I hope so," Zero said, scanning the figures in the parking area. They supposed most of the people there looked ordinary enough, but there was a clump of three Orions who strolled between the vehicles, studying each one carefully. Their expressions reminded Zero of the way the Watchers at Tars Lamora would inspect the chimerium that was mined each day. Like they were sizing up the vehicles, trying to decide how much they could sell each piece for.

"Will our vehicle be safe here?" Zero drifted toward the front seat.

"Yeah," Dal said, eyeing the same Orions that Zero had spotted. "Better leave the shields up while we're gone."

"Can do!" Jankom tapped on the controllers, and although the vehicle's engine died, there was still a faint thrum as the shields remained in place. "Everybody out!"

Dal burst from the vehicle first, standing with his hands on his hips, breathing in the cool, crisp air of Odaru. It smelled like tree sap and energy shields and bahgol, a kind of Klingon tea that Dal had tried once. Not that different from any of the markets he'd visited with Nandi.

Jankom followed, bouncing with excitement as he took in the scene. "Look at this place!" he said. "Jankom Pog bets you could build a whole starship just from parts you bought here."

"Stolen parts," Zero muttered as they floated out of the vehicle. "Perhaps we shouldn't dally too long."

"I thought you wanted to see a thieves' market," Dal said, giving Zero a playful nudge. "You don't want to stick around? Enjoy the sights?"

"Eat some Tellarite mud stew?" Jankom added. "Jankom Pog can smell it from here. MmMmm!"

"We do have a mission," Zero said. "We mustn't let ourselves be distracted."

"I agree with Zero," Rok-Tahk said. She was the last to step out of the vehicle, her heart pounding furiously in her chest. Under ordinary circumstances, she might have liked to look around the market a bit—there was a sign advertising a chance to pet an Earth cat that looked particularly promising—but under normal circumstances, she wouldn't have to carry around a replicated ground vehicle battery either.

"You two are no fun," Dal said. "Come on, let's go!"

They walked together up the footpath leading to the market. People buzzed around them, a dizzying array of different species. The universal translators they wore could hardly keep up with all the different languages in the market, so snippets of unfamiliar words slipped through.

Dal stopped them when they arrived at the entrance. Rok-Tahk marveled at what was before them—a huge arch of energy that cycled through WELCOME TO ORGORA MARKET written in Federation Standard, Ferengi, Klingon, and dozens of other languages Rok-Tahk didn't recognize. She squeezed the battery close to her chest as people swarmed around their little group, flooding into the crowded market.

"We've got a lot of ground to cover," Dal said. "Let's fan out, but we should keep each other in sight so no one gets lost."

Rok-Tahk let out a sigh of relief; she was sure he was about to send them in on their own.

"If you see anyone that looks like they might be willing to trade, let me know," Dal said. "I'll check 'em out and see what I think."

Zero and Rok-Tahk both nodded, pressing closer together, but Jankom was bouncing around the entrance brimming with excitement. "Let's get in there!" he said, his eyes huge. He whipped around and grinned at the group. "Jankom Pog does not want to be Jankom Pog while we're here," he added.

"Okay." Dal frowned. "As long as we find the phase—"

"Jankom Pog will be the famous trader Fafnir Avant!" he continued, posing with his chest puffed out. "He travels the galaxy, searching for treasure—that he's willing to sell, for a price." Jankom's eyes glittered.

"Okay, fine," Dal said. "Whatever. Let's get looking."

And all four members of the crew stepped into the market.

Somehow, the din was even louder once they passed under the entrance arch. Dal and Jankom led the way, each one branching off to opposite sides of the path. Rok-Tahk and Zero pressed close together, trailing down the center. The street was lined with open-air buildings crammed with different vendors, all of them organized in no reasonable order that Zero could see. A booth selling some bright blue Romulan drink was cozied up next to a woman selling bolts of brightly colored fabric. Beside her was a man hunched over a split-apart computer, its innards glittering in the sunlight.

"Hey!" Jankom bounded over to Zero and Rok-Tahk. "Rok-Tahk, come with Fafnir."

"Who?" She squeezed the battery case closer to her chest.

"Jankom Pog," he hissed sharply. Then he straightened up. "Fafnir Avant, the greatest treasure hunter—"

"I'd rather stay with Dal," she said. Then she immediately felt a surge of panic—where was Dal? Her eyes flew across the crowd until she spotted a flash of Dal's gray hair next to an electronics booth.

"No, Fafnir needs a bodyguard."

"A what?"

But Jankom was already tugging her by the hand, pulling her toward a stand dripping with holographic jewelry. "A bodyguard," he said. "But he shouldn't speak—"

"I'm a girl!" Rok-Tahk shouted.

Jankom rolled his eyes. "Okay, fine. *She* shouldn't speak. Just stand behind Fafnir like this." He crossed his hands over his chest and scowled.

Rok-Tahk glared at him.

"Exactly! Perfect!"

"Jankom, I—"

"No talking!" Jankom whirled around, heading toward the jewelry booth. Rok-Tahk swallowed her anger and turned to Zero—but Zero had vanished! She froze as people bustled around her, an overwhelming sea of strangers. She scanned the market, looking for Dal or Zero, only to be jostled by someone pushing a cart overflowing with cuts of meat.

"Don't block the road!" the vendor shouted at her.

"I—I'm sorry," she said, trying desperately not to cry. She still couldn't see Dal or Zero, but Jankom was waving wildly at her only a few paces away. She bolted toward him, hardly paying attention to where she was going. She was so focused on getting to Jankom, in fact, that she ran into *another* stranger, this one wearing a long black coat. This time, the case carrying the battery flew out from her side. Rok-Tahk yelped and grabbed at it, pulling it close to her chest. She patted wildly at the case and let out a long breath of relief that she could still feel the battery inside.

"Thank goodness," she whispered as she darted over to Jankom.

"Remember," he told her. "No talking."

Then he marched up to the booth of blinking, shimmering jewelry. The trader there was a wan-looking Romulan who blinked dolefully down at him.

"What's the matter?" Jankom shouted dramatically, planting his feet wide. "Don't you recognize the great Fafnir Avant?"

"Who?" said the trader.

"Fafnir Avant," Jankom said. "The greatest treasure hunter in four quadrants."

"Never heard of him," the trader said. "You want to buy something or not?"

Jankom rubbed his chin as he marched down the display of jewelry. "This is all trash," he said. "Furi! Come with me!"

He whipped away from the jewelry seller, but Rok-Tahk made no move to follow him, just stood admiring the jewelry displays as they cycled through their different settings. It was so pretty, the way the sunlight caught on the brilliantly colored jewels.

"Furi!" he hissed, and Rok-Tahk blinked over at him.

"Oh," she said. "You mean—"

"You're mute!" he reminded her.

Rok-Tahk rolled her eyes, but she did follow him deeper into the crush of the market. It was better to play Jankom's mute bodyguard Furi than to be alone among all this chaos.

On the other side of the market street, Dal and Zero strode past different vendors. Dal frowned, frustrated: all of these shops were much too respectable for what they were trying to do. Most of them were just selling food anyway, and as delicious as they smelled, the crew wasn't on Odaru to eat.

"Do you still have eyes on Jankom and Rok-Tahk?" Dal asked Zero, who drifted alongside him.

"Yes," Zero answered. "They're only a few booths away."

Dal nodded. The last thing they needed was to get genuinely separated. This place was huge. Dal and Zero kept going. As they ventured further into the market, it was clear that this place deserved its reputation as a place for thieves.

"What exactly are you looking for?" Zero asked. "Perhaps I can help." They swiveled around in midair. "I do have a wider range than you, Dal."

Dal grinned. "Maybe, but you don't have the eye for criminality."

"I beg to differ. I—"

Dal waved Zero off. "Seriously, it's hard to explain. But someone who's willing to make a deal, they always have this glint in their eye. It's kind of like desperation—but not exactly."

"I see." Zero rotated slowly, scanning the crowds. Their gaze passed over Jankom and Rok-Tahk, who had left a booth advertising firecrackers and were crossing the street toward Dal and Zero. "I think the others are headed this way."

Dal gave only a grunt of acknowledgment. Zero continued to scan the crowd. It felt like its own life-form, moving as sinuously as a snake down the narrow street. A few faces stood out: there was a particularly large Klingon who strode to the center of the path, a tiny yipping animal marching alongside his massive legs. A pair of Orion dancers swirled and spun as they made their way down the path, and the crowd parted for them, delighted cheers trailing along the dancers' path. And that catlike Caitian in the purple cloak—

"Hail the others," Dal hissed. "I've found someone."

Zero spun back around and floated alongside Dal. "Where?"

"Straight ahead. But don't be too obvious." Dal's eyes glittered. "There's a Caitian woman in a purple coat. Do you see her?"

Zero zoomed their focus up ahead. "I do! But she just turned down that alley."

"We need to follow her." Dal surged forward, tapping lightly on his combadge. "Jankom. Rok-Tahk. Get over here now."

Jankom's voice spilled over the comm: *"There's no Jankom here. Only Fafnir Avant!"*

"Then Fafnir Avant needs to get over here now."

Dal moved quickly, slipping deftly through a pair of women haggling over the cost of formal gowns, then clipping around the corner booth belonging to a Ferengi selling jewel-colored drinks.

"*Slow down!*" Rok-Tahk said over the comm. "*We can't keep up.*"

"Meet me at the side alley. Zero knows what I'm talking about."

The alley in question appeared up ahead. Dal dived into it, his heart racing. He swept his gaze around, looking for the Caitian in the purple coat. When Dal spotted her earlier, she'd been walking quickly, one paw pressed protectively over her left pocket. She had something she shouldn't, and she clearly wanted to unload it.

The sound of scraping metal echoed down the alley—and Dal saw a door hanging open at the far end. He saw the Caitian woman in the purple coat.

She disappeared inside.

"Dal! Why'd you run off like that?" It was Rok-Tahk, coming to stand beside him. Jankom and Zero were with her.

"You see that door up there?" Dal asked. "That's where we need to go."

"You're sure?" Rok-Tahk frowned and squeezed the battery case close to her chest.

"Positive. Someone's buying illegal goods in there." He grinned. "I told you I could spot 'em anywhere."

"Illegal?" Zero cried. "Look at all these vendors! Why do we need to go someplace that's selling illegal goods?"

Dal sighed, annoyed. "We need to go someplace that'll fly under the Federation's radar."

"But we aren't doing anything wrong," Rok-Tahk said. "And we certainly aren't doing anything *illegal*."

"You heard Janeway." Dal frowned. "The Federation wouldn't approve of using the vehicle replicator to make a battery to sell. So it's better to go someplace that won't keep the best records. Just in case."

Rok-Tahk and Zero glanced at each other. Zero could feel Rok-Tahk's doubt for just a second before they slipped out of her head. As a Medusan, Zero could read thoughts, but they tried to avoid doing it with their crewmates.

Jankom, though, had no qualms about the questionable vendor Dal had in mind.

"Fafnir Avant is ready to make a trade," Jankom announced, rubbing his hands together deviously. "Bodyguard! You go first!"

"I'm not your ridiculous bodyguard," Rok-Tahk snapped.

"Stop arguing. Let's find out what's behind that door." Dal moved forward. Both Rok-Tahk and Jankom heard the urgency in his voice, and they did the same.

Zero also understood the urgency, but something prickled at them inside their containment suit. It felt like a stray thought from the crowd, directed in the group's direction.

They looked back at the alley entrance, not sure what they expected to see. It was empty, the crowd of customers rushing past on the main street.

Zero sighed softly, then glided forward. The others were almost at the door. And that's when Zero heard it—

A faint rustling. They whipped around.

This time, they saw the flutter of a black cloak vanish around the edge of the alley's entrance.

CHAPTER FOUR

"I can't believe I have to stay behind," Gwyn said, draping herself dramatically over the captain's chair.

"Staying behind with the ship is an important role," Janeway said. "And you *do* know it's typically officers who stay behind."

"So Dal should have stayed!" Gwyn shook her head. "It's so unfair! Dal had an actual life before he was sold to my father. I had never even left Tars Lamora before we found the ship." She straightened up in her seat and turned to Janeway. "He even told us how he'd been to so many markets like Orgora. Why not let me have a chance to explore a bit?"

Janeway smiled. "He has a point about having

experience. His background with Nandi means he knows what to look for."

"Yeah, but how am I ever going to get any experience if I'm stuck on the *Protostar* the whole time?"

A gurgle drifted up from under the control panel. Gwyn ducked down to find Murf gliding toward her, his big eyes sad.

"You wanted to see the market too, didn't you?"

Murf broke into a big smile and made a sort of slurping sound.

"See?" Gwyn sat back up in her seat. Murf crawled his way up to the armrest and gurgled in agreement. "He doesn't like getting left behind either."

Janeway smiled. "Can I be honest with you, Gwyn?"

Gwyn sighed. "Another lecture about my responsibility to my ship?"

"No." Janeway walked over to the captain's chair and knelt beside it. Murf sniffed at her hologram. "I was going to say you remind me a bit of myself."

"I do?" Gwyn leaned forward, intrigued.

"Well, my real-world self. Not my hologram self." Janeway chuckled. "I was like you when I was an ensign. Always volunteering to go on any away mission I could." She dropped her voice to a conspiratorial whisper. "And perhaps going on more than I should have when I was captain of *Voyager*."

Gwyn smiled. Something about Janeway seeing herself in Gwyn made Gwyn feel comforted.

"Maybe you can watch the ship on your own," Gwyn said mischievously.

Janeway arched an eyebrow. "Maybe I can."

"Really?" Gwyn leaped from her seat, her heart fluttering in excitement. Murf chirped alongside her. "Can Murf come with me?"

"Probably for the best," Janeway said. "I'm not sure I could stop him from eating the entire bridge."

Both she and Gwyn looked down at Murf, who gazed guilelessly up at them.

"Thank you so much," Gwyn said. "I can't tell you how much I appreciate this!"

"Go," said Janeway. "But keep your combadge on you. You never know when you might need it."

Twenty minutes later, Gwyn was staring up at the massive arch marking the entrance of Orgora Market, watching as it repeated W ELCOME over and over in dozens of different languages. Gwyn had studied almost all of them back at her home on Tars Lamora, where she'd helped her father communicate with his many prisoners.

"That was Ferengi," she said excitedly to Murf. "And Caitian. And—wow, I think that's Bolian?" She smiled down at him. "I'd just started studying it before we left."

Murf trilled, wiggling his gelatinous head back and forth.

"Okay, okay. I know. Let's go check it out." Gwyn made her expression serious. "And stay next to me. No wandering off and eating anything, okay?"

Murf only smiled in response.

They passed under the arch, stepping into the flow of customers surging down the street. Buildings rose up like cliffs on either side of them, the windows all lit up with signs for the treasures that waited inside. But booths crowded around the outside of the buildings too, trinkets and gadgets glittering in the sun.

"Wow," Gwyn breathed. "Look at this place."

Murf bumped his head up against her hand, then began gliding toward a nearby booth stacked high with wooden sculptures.

"Murf! I said no wandering off!" Gwyn jogged behind him, catching up just as he reached the booth.

"Welcome," said the vendor, a woman with a ridged nose and friendly smile. Her earring caught the sunlight, and Gwyn recognized it immediately: she was a Bajoran.

"Hello!" Gwyn said cheerfully in the Bajoran language.

"Ah, you speak my language?" the woman said.

Gwyn nodded and answered in the language, "I taught myself."

"Impressive!" The vendor beamed at her. "It's been so long since I've heard Bajoran here on Odaru. Please, look around." She gestured down at her display of statues. "Traditional Bajoran religious iconography," she explained. "That always pulls people in. But I have a whole variety of treasures inside my shop proper."

Murf lifted himself up, eyeing the statues.

"We'll see what you have inside," Gwyn said. "Thank you so much!"

Gwyn pulled Murf away from the statues, dragging him through the beaded curtain marking the entrance of the shop.

47

Inside felt like an entirely different world. The clamor of the crowd outside was muffled, and the air was dark, cool, and smelled faintly of sweet, dark spices. Unlike the neat display of statues outside, everything inside was crammed wherever it could fit, a chaos of trinkets, electronic equipment, and dusty old antiques.

"Murf! No!" Gwyn darted after her friend, who had started to chew on the corner of a tapestry hanging from the wall. "You can't eat anything here," she whispered to him. "Otherwise, we'll have to pay for it."

Murf frowned, and to her relief, let go of the tapestry.

"Just look," she said. "No touching anything. Okay?"

They wove through the shop together. There was no order to the displays that Gwyn could see: a set of crystal dishware sat on a shelf beside a precarious stack of old-fashioned communication PADDs, behind which rose an enormous carved statue of some kind of strange animal Gwyn didn't recognize. There was a rack overflowing with traditional Bajoran clothes, and on the wall behind it, a holographic painting of the Crab Nebula.

"This place is amazing," Gwyn breathed, pushing her way toward the back of the shop, where she found an entire wall lined with glass jars filled with dried plants. Murf followed alongside her, gaping in wonder. He did not, to Gwyn's great relief, try to eat anything else.

Gwyn gazed up at the shelves of plants. Each one was labeled neatly in Bajoran—a blend of spices and flowers. She wondered what they were used for, but there was no one in the shop to ask.

Something glinted in the corner of Gwyn's eye: another shelf, this one lined with metal trinkets. The shop was so crowded, she'd missed this shelf—in fact, it felt like every time she looked around, she saw something new.

"Come on, Murf. Let's see what's over here." She patted him on the top of his head, drawing him after her. Most of the trinkets on the shelf looked like spare electronics parts, some of which had been affixed together to create dolls.

Gwyn lifted one of the dolls, staring down at its simple metallic face. It wore a dress of silk scraps, and its hair was a nest of fine, dead filament, all twisted together into a braid.

"Do you like it?"

Gwyn jumped and nearly dropped the doll. "Oh!" she said. "You startled me."

She turned around to find the shopkeeper smiling down at her and Murf. "My assistant is watching the booth outside," the shopkeeper said. "And I thought I'd check on you two." She gave Murf a pointed look.

"We're just looking around." Gwyn felt herself blush as she set the doll back on the shelf. "We don't have much in the way of payment."

The shopkeeper smiled. "If you want the doll, you can have it. No payment."

"Really?" Gwyn looked back over at it. Her father had never let her play with dolls—with any toys— when she was growing up. Her whole life, he had been training her. And of course she didn't want a doll *now*. She was too old for it. But Rok-Tahk might like it. And it might look nice propped up in Gwyn's quarters.

"Of course." The shopkeeper picked it up and smoothed down the braid. "An artist in the city makes these out of old starship parts and other odds and ends. I've always found them charming." She handed the doll to Gwyn. "And it's been so lovely to talk with someone in Bajoran."

Gwyn squeezed the doll to her chest. She'd studied languages to help her father communicate with his prisoners but had come to love the process for itself. That it could eventually lead to her getting a gift from a Bajoran shopkeeper on a distant planet—

Well, Gwyn was as surprised as anyone at the direction her life had taken.

"Thank you," she said.

"Come back anytime," the shopkeeper said.

Gwyn thanked her again, then she and Murf stepped out of the cool, dark space, back into the brilliant noise and chaos of the market.

CHAPTER FIVE

"I still don't think we should go in there." Rok-Tahk stared at the big metal door set into the stone building. "There's no sign or anything. How do we even know it's a shop?"

"It's probably not a shop," Dal said. "But there's someone in there who's willing to trade with us. Trust me."

"I don't like this," Rok-Tahk said nervously.

"I don't either." Zero zipped back over to the group, a faint tremor in their voice. "Plus, I think someone's watching us."

Zero pointed to the opening of the alley, and the whole group turned to look. No one was there.

"It's fine," Dal said. "Come on, let's get inside."

He stepped up to the door and pulled it open, the

metal grinding and groaning. Inside, faint twinkling music played softly, but it was too dark for Dal to see much else.

"Hello?" he called out, stepping across the doorway. "Is there anyone here?"

He had stepped into a small, dim room. It looked like a waiting room—it was empty save for a few tattered chairs, and there was a door set into the far wall.

Dal stuck his head back outside. "It's fine," he said. "Come on!"

Jankom bounded in first, his heavy feet clomping on the floor. "Fafnir Avant is here!" he bellowed.

Dal rolled his eyes, went up to the closed door, and knocked twice. "Hello?" he called out. "We have some—"

The door swung open, and a towering woman stepped into the doorway. Her long black hair was teased up over her fierce, bony face, and two tusks jutted sideways out of her mouth.

"Yes?" she said sharply. "What do you want?"

Dal took a deep breath—the woman might be intimidating, but he and his crew were here for a reason. "We're looking to trade," he said, straightening his shoulders.

The woman arched an eyebrow. "Is that so? Well, I am a trader." She pressed her hand to her heart and gave a shallow bow. "My name is Teyless. And you—"

"Tad," Dal lied. "My friends and I—we're looking for a transporter phase coil."

Teyless broke into a wide grin. "Ah. I think we may be able to help each other, then. Come. Join me."

She stepped back through the doorway, disappearing into the shadows. Dal turned and gestured to the others.

"Come on," he whispered.

"Are you sure about this?" Jankom said, his eyes wide.

"She said she has phase coils! Come on."

"Technically," Zero said. "She said she might be able to help us—"

Dal rolled his eyes. "Rok-Tahk, come with me."

Rok-Tahk sighed and shuffled forward, the battery case cradled in one hand.

"What's taking so long?" Teyless reappeared in the doorway, her gaze sharp as she looked around at the crew. "You said you wanted to trade. Let's trade."

"Nothing's wrong!" Dal whirled around to face

Teyless, who glowered down at him. "We were just coming. Weren't we?"

Teyless fixed the crew with a dark, searing glare. Dal was relieved when he heard the shuffle of feet behind him as he began to move toward the door.

Teyless stepped aside to let him pass, and he walked into a large room—it felt to Dal like the storage bay on the *Protostar*. Most of the space was taken up by large, unmarked crates, and figures shuffled around the room, scanning the crates with PADDs and then loading the crates onto a small transporter platform.

The others stepped into the room behind Dal. Rok-Tahk clutched the case as tightly as she could, feeling overwhelmed by the size of the space. Zero stuck close beside her, concerned when they saw the group wasn't entering an actual shop, but rather some kind of storage facility. Even Jankom stayed quiet, deciding it was better to keep Fafnir Avant tucked away for the time being.

"Come. Have a seat." Teyless led them all over to a desk shoved up against a far wall, near the transporter. There were only two chairs set up in front of the desk. Jankom grabbed one immediately, his eyes on the transporter. Teyless's associates had just loaded up one of those unmarked crates, and it shimmered away, the air chiming in its wake. Its phase coils were working properly, then.

"Where are you sending those things?" Jankom asked.

Teyless glared at him. "That's of no concern to you."

"Of course not!" Dal slid into the other empty chair, a bright grin plastered on his face. Teyless fixed her glare onto him. "You can ignore him. He's just like that."

"Hey!" Jankom shouted. "What does that mean?"

Zero flitted up to Jankom. "It's probably best we keep quiet," they said softly, gently patting Jankom's knee with one hand.

"Jankom Pog was just curious," Jankom muttered back.

Dal took a deep breath, hoping that was the end of it. Teyless leaned back in the chair, her arms crossed over her chest. "You said you need a phase coil," she said. "What do you have to trade for it?"

Dal swallowed, then glanced over at Rok-Tahk. Her eyes were wide with fear.

"A Starfleet-issued ground vehicle battery," he said, speaking with a confidence he didn't feel. "Never used."

"Never used?" Teyless's eyes went wide. "And how did you come across such a thing?"

Dal could feel the others watching him, waiting for his response. Tayless folded her hands over her stomach, her expression mocking.

Beside him, Jankom shifted in his chair, and that's when Dal was struck with inspiration.

"A treasure hunter never reveals his secrets," he said.

"It's true!" Jankom started, but Dal shot out his arm and squeezed his wrist, stopping him from saying anything else.

"Treasure hunters, huh?" Teyless chuckled. "So you're thieves."

"We're not thieves!" Rok-Tahk said indignantly. Dal whipped his head around to shush her.

"Thieves, treasure hunters, defected Starfleet officers? I don't care." Teyless tossed her long black hair over her shoulder. "I know how to be discreet. I'd like to see this vehicle battery."

Dal hesitated. He'd been in enough negotiations

with people of questionable ethics to know he needed to tread carefully.

"My associate here has the battery tucked away for safekeeping." Dal patted Rok-Tahk on the arm, and she looked over at him nervously. He nodded at her, then at the carrier.

"Oh," Rok-Tahk said. "Yes. It's in here." She lifted the case and reached for the latch. "Should I—"

"Not yet." Dal leaned forward, over Teyless's desk.

"I want to see the phase coil first," he said. "Then we'll show you the battery."

Teyless stared at him for a long moment. Dal fidgeted, certain she was going to throw him—and the rest of his crew—back out on the street.

But then she let out a loud, shrieking laugh.

"Smart," she said. "You know what you're doing." She snapped her fingers and shouted over at the people loading the crates onto the transporter. "Transporter coil! Now!"

One of the workers, a Klingon, immediately walked over to a stack of crates on the other side of the warehouse, pried one open, and pulled out a small metal device. He set it on Teyless's desk.

"That's it!" Jankom shouted. "That's what we need!"

Dal hissed at him to be quiet.

Teyless chuckled. "I told you that we'd be able to help each other. Now." She yanked the phase coil away from Jankom, who was reaching out to grab it. He gave a soft groan of disappointment. Dal just hoped she wouldn't hold it against them.

"Let's see that battery." Her eyes glittered. "If it really is in as good a condition as you claim, I'll be happy to hand over this phase coil. Brand new. Manufactured right here on Odaru."

"The battery's in perfect condition," Dal said, his heart fluttering excitedly in his chest. The plan was all falling into place. He turned to Rok-Tahk. "If you would be so kind."

Rok-Tahk nodded and looped the case up over her head. She settled it in her lap and pulled open the lid—

And then immediately snapped it shut again.

"Um," she said, terror coursing inside her. *Just a trick of the light. It's dark in here.*

"Any time now," Dal said through his strained smile.

Rok-Tahk stared down at the case. She could feel tears forming behind her eyes.

"Rok-Tahk," Dal hissed angrily.

With a soft, miserable whine, Rok-Tahk lifted the lid up and held the case over so Dal could see inside.

The battery was gone. In its place was a pile of stones and scrap metal.

"What's going on?" snarled Teyless, drawing herself over the desk. "Where's the battery?"

"It's, um, well—" But Dal wasn't fast enough to come up with an excuse. Teyless's hand snapped out and grabbed the case, dragging it over the desk. When she saw what was inside, she let out a fearsome shriek of rage.

"How *dare* you?" she roared, throwing the case across the room. It landed with a clatter, the rubble spilling out across the floor.

"The battery!" Jankom yelled. "Jankom Pog repli—"

Dal elbowed him hard in the side. "It was in there," he said quickly. "I swear to you. My associate here, she never let it out of her sight!"

Teyless fixed her fearsome gaze onto Rok-Tahk, who cringed backward, whimpering. "I-it's true!" she stammered. "I d-don't understand—"

Zero fluttered over beside her, stroking her

shoulder. "It's okay," they murmured softly, thinking again about the flutter of a black cloak they saw in the alley, right before they stepped into Teyless's warehouse.

"You wasted my time!" Teyless roared. "And no one wastes the time of Teyless Usk'is!"

She launched herself over the table and grabbed Dal's arm, yanking him to his feet. Before he could so much as shout in surprise, the workers swarmed around his crew, grabbing them as roughly as Teyless had grabbed him. He realized, with a slow dread, that they must have been watching their conversation the whole time, ready to act the second it went wrong.

"Tie them up," Teyless ordered. "We'll show them what happens when you try to cheat me."

"We weren't trying to cheat you!" Dal shouted, struggling against her grip.

"It's true!" Zero shouted, flailing against their own captor. "Someone was following us. They must have done something—"

Zero's captor looped an energy cord around Zero's containment unit, making it sputter and spark.

"Hey!" Dal said. "Don't hurt them!"

The captor just snarled in response. Teyless jerked on Dal's arm, dragging him deeper into the warehouse. Teyless's subordinates had made quick work of Jankom and Rok-Tahk, both of them wrapped in glowing energy ropes. Suddenly, Dal felt the sizzle of energy on his own skin.

"Hey!" he shouted, trying to wriggle free. But Teyless had already looped the rope completely around his wrists.

"I think some time in the golden crate will be good for you," Teyless said with a smirk.

"The what?" Fear lanced though Dal's chest. Teyless tugged on the rope, forcing him to trip after her. The others were dragged along behind him. Jankom shouted his protests, thrashing against his bindings. Zero sputtered against the energy ropes, still trying to quietly plead with their captor to let all of them go. Rok-Tahk was crying softly, stumbling along after her own captor.

Too late, Dal realized he should have called to Gwyn on his communicator badge. But with his bound hands, he couldn't even do that.

"The golden crate," Teyless said proudly, jerking Dal around.

The "crate" wasn't a crate at all, but a cage, and it wasn't golden, either, although it was a kind of burnished, coppery color. It had clearly been made from welding together scrap parts and old metal that had been melted down and remolded, and the effect was that it looked lumpen, distorted, and terrible.

Teyless slammed open the door and threw Dal inside. Jankom came rolling in next, scrambling to his feet as soon as he could. Like Dal, his hands were bound behind his back.

"You'll regret this!" Jankom shouted. "You'll regret throwing Jankom Pog in this piece of old garbage!"

Zero flew in and landed with a shudder on the ground, their containment unit still sputtering from the rope.

Rok-Tahk trudged in last. She looked down at the others with wet eyes. "I'm sorry," she said in a small voice. "I don't know what happened."

Teyless banged the door shut, hard enough that the entire cage rattled. She locked it with a slim metal key that activated an energy shield, which exploded around the perimeter of the cage. Dal could hear it thrumming.

"We can get you another battery!" he shouted, but Teyless only laughed. She lifted up one hand, the key dangling from her finger.

"No," she said. "I think this is a much better trade."

CHAPTER SIX

Dal watched Jankom fling himself against the bars of the cage, making the whole thing rattle. He'd been doing it for the past ten minutes, ever since Teyless hung the key to the cage's lock on the wall, just out of reach. Not that any of them could reach the key with their hands tied.

And that was the *real* reason Jankom was making such a racket—to distract from what Dal was doing.

"Let us out!" Jankom shouted dramatically, slamming his body against the cage so hard, the back lifted up. Dal held his bound hands positioned just right so that the sharp side of one of the bars there snagged on the rope.

"It's working," he whispered. "Keep at it."

"Free us!" Jankom bellowed.

"Yes, please!" Rok-Tahk wedged her shoulder up against the cage with enough force that it scraped across the floor. Dal felt his rope splinter even farther.

Teyless stood over by the transporter, barking orders at her crew as they continued to transport crate after crate. But when she heard the cage scraping along the floor, she whipped her head over.

Dal froze, keeping his hands tied behind his back.

"You two are making an awful racket," Teyless said coldly. She loped toward them, her face twisted in anger. "It's making it very hard for my crew to concentrate on their work."

The crew in question stared dolefully over at the cage.

"Then let us out," Jankom said. "Jankom Pog can make you a new battery—"

"Jankom," Zero gasped, but Teyless chuckled.

"*Make* me a new battery?" She arched an eyebrow, the anger in her expression washing over into amusement. "Is that all you think the *Protostar* is good for?"

Every single one of them, Dal and Rok-Tahk,

Jankom and Zero, froze in place. Dal could feel the others looking over at him, could feel their confusion staining the air.

Teyless grinned, her tusks gleaming. "I suppose there's no harm in telling you now." As she marched over to the cage, she grabbed a chair and dragged it with her, swinging it around to position it directly in front of where Rok-Tahk was still pressed against the cage bars. Teyless sat down, leaning back, with one leg propped haphazardly on the cage. When Jankom lunged at her, she kicked it away, laughing.

"How do you know about our—about the *Protostar*?" Dal stood up, arranging his hand so the ropes would pass over the sharp, jagged edge of the bar one last time. To his relief, he felt the rope snap and fall away. He grabbed the loose end before it could dangle down, and he kept his hands behind him.

It was something, to have even this small thing work out in his favor. As soon as Teyless looked away, he'd be able to get the others' hands untied too.

Teyless tilted her head to the side, eyes glittering.

"Well, T'agross there detected your ship's warp signature when you landed on Odaru." She gestured over at one of her crew, a tall, lanky Klingon who snarled a little at the mention of his name. "We have a whole setup in the back, looking for interesting ships to plunder."

Off to Dal's side, Zero let out a loud gasp, and Dal felt the same sickening dread. "You were tracking us all along," Zero said. "Weren't you?"

Teyless grinned. Then she jumped to her feet and walked off.

"They know about the *Protostar!*" Rok-Tahk cried, whirling around. "What are we going to do?"

Dal fought back his own sense of terror and gave Rok-Tahk, and the others, a rakish smile. He glanced over at Teyless, who had pried open one of the crates sitting next to her desk. Angling himself behind Rok-Tahk, he showed his crew his untied hands.

"It wo—" Jankom started to yell, but Rok-Tahk nudged him hard enough that he quickly fell silent.

"Yes, but don't let them know," Dal said. Teyless had pulled something out of the crate and turned back toward the cage. "Quick, she's coming back over here."

Dal quickly rearranged his hands behind his back again, just as Teyless came striding over to the cage, and sat down in the chair. As soon as she'd approached, he saw what she had pulled out of the crate.

"Our battery!" Rok-Tahk cried. "How did you—"

"Oh, give it a think," Teyless said, her grin sharp and cruel. "I'm sure even you can figure it out."

"Don't speak to her like that!" Zero said, zipping over to Rok-Tahk's side. But Rok-Tahk *had* figured it out. She'd been running after Jankom in the market. Someone had bumped her, and the case flew out of her hands.

"It was just a second," she whispered. "And the case never left my sight! How—"

Teyless made a clicking sound, and one of her crew, a lizardy-looking fellow in a black coat, let out a high yipping noise that might have been laughter. T'agross, the Klingon, joined in.

"Micro-transporter," Teyless said sharply. Her crew's laughter stopped. She pointed at the man in the dark coat. "Ioma there just had to get the case away from you long enough to transport the battery into my office. T'agross was waiting to transport the rocks a second later. That"—her grin widened—"is how we did it."

"That black coat!" Zero cried, fluttering up to the edge of the cage. "Ioma was following us, wasn't he? Into the alley?"

Teyless nodded. "You're a smart one, Medusan. I had him follow you in case Chadossa wasn't enough to lure you in. Which reminds me." She leaned back her head. "Chadossa! You can come out now. We've got them."

Not a single one of Dal's crewmates was surprised when the Caitian woman in the purple coat burst through one of the far doors.

"But Ioma didn't need to be there, did he?" she said, her whiskers bristling. "I told you I could handle the job on my own."

Ioma hissed something at her, and she hissed back. Whatever they said wasn't recognized by the crew's translators.

"Yes, yes, you did marvelously," Teyless said, sounding annoyed. "Now put this battery back in the case."

Chadossa strutted over, looking, Dal thought, immensely pleased with herself. She gave him a wink as she plucked the battery out of Teyless's hand. "If you think my little act in the market was good," she purred, "wait until you see how fast I strip your ship."

"What!" Dal squawked, surging forward—and remembering at the last minute that his hands were still supposed to be tied. "No," he said, more calmly, keeping his arms stuck close behind him. "You'll never get aboard the *Protostar*."

Teyless and Chadossa glanced at each other for a moment, then burst into laughter. "How exactly do you plan to do to stop us?" Teyless said.

"How do you plan to get aboard?" Dal countered. "You really think we'd leave our ship completely unprotected?"

"This isn't our first time raiding a ship," Teyless said, rising from her chair. "And the fact of the matter is that you are currently locked in a cage, hands tied, key"—she nodded toward where the key hung on the wall—"just out of reach, while all we have to do is get past your shields." Teyless bared her teeth, a smile that was more of a threat than anything else. "I think we have the upper hand."

She whirled away, marching back over to her

desk. Chadossa gave Dal and his crew one last smirk before following, her tail whipping around after her.

For half a second, everyone was quiet. Then they all immediately turned around to Dal.

"What are we going to do?" Jankom cried, looking more miserable than ever.

"I can't believe I let them steal the battery," Rok-Tahk said, shoulders slumped. "It was only a second! And I checked it!"

"It wasn't your fault," Zero said gently. "The same thing could have happened to any of us."

"Who cares about the battery?" Jankom shouted. "The ship! We have to figure out what to do about the ship!"

"Keep your voice down," Dal said, flicking his gaze over to Teyless. Thankfully, she, and the rest of her gang, seemed to be ignoring them. But Dal knew that didn't mean they weren't listening in.

He lifted his gaze to the worried faces of his crew. "Be quiet," he said. "And act normal. Rok-Tahk, move over to the left a little."

"Why?" She blinked in confusion.

Dal grinned up at her. "Just trust me, okay? But I

need you to block their view for a second."

"Oh." Rok-Tahk shuffled over to the left-hand corner of the cage. "Is that—"

"Perfect. Jankom, come over here on her right."

Jankom did as he was asked without so much as a peep, for which Dal was extremely grateful.

"What should I do?" Zero asked.

"Come fill in the gap there." Dal nodded in approval as Zero slid into place. Now that he was hidden by his friends, he finally brought his hands around in front of him.

"Don't act weird!" he reminded them in a short, sharp voice, cutting off at least one delighted gasp from Rok-Tahk.

"I still can't believe that worked," she said happily.

"Jankom Pog knows how to throw his weight around." Jankom nudged Rok-Tahk's side. She just scowled in response.

"Don't move," Dal said. "But, Jankom, I need you to start shouting about something."

"What?" Jankom frowned. "You told Jankom Pog to be quiet!"

"I know. But I can't have the traders hearing Gwyn's voice, can I?" And with a triumphant flourish,

Dal whipped his combadge out of his pocket. "So I need you to make some racket. Nothing that'll bring them over here, but enough that they won't hear her when she responds."

"Ah! Now that, Jankom Pog can do." Immediately, he banged his multi-mitt on the cage bars. "We'll never get out of here!" he wailed. "And now we're stuck on this crummy planet!"

"Agreed!" Zero said, joining in on the clamor. They were much more soft-spoken than Jankom, but every little bit helped, and when Rok-Tahk chimed in with a perfectly pitched, "I want to go home!" Dal knew it was time to act.

He hit the combadge and held it up to his mouth so he could speak in a whisper. "Gwyn," he said. "Answer me. We've got a problem. Gwyn."

He held the badge up to his ear, waiting. His heart hammered fast in his chest. "Gwyn?" he hissed.

Then her voice came through, faint but clear. "*Dal?*"

He breathed with relief and sneaked a glance over at Rok-Tahk, who had taken to fake crying about being locked in the cage. A perfect cover. Teyless wasn't paying the cage any attention, either, just digging through one of the crates.

"I don't have time to explain," he said softly, ducking back behind Rok-Tahk. "But you need to be ready. Some traders—they saw the *Protostar*'s energy signature. They want to raid the ship."

He held the combadge by his ear. There was no response. "Gwyn!" he said, a little more loudly than he should have.

Over the din of his crewmates, Dal heard Teyless calling out to her subordinates: "Bring the pulse rifles!"

Dal brought the combadge back down to his mouth.

"Gwyn, answer me!" he said. "They're going to—"

"*I'm not at the ship.*" Gwyn's voice came through, tinny and small. Dal froze, looking up at the others in a panic. It was clear from their expressions that they had heard too.

"*I'm sorry,*" Gwyn said. "*I came down to the market. Murf's with me.*"

Dal curled his hand around the combadge, muffling Gwyn's voice as the voices of the others drifted into silence.

"Did Jankom Pog hear that right?" Jankom stared at Dal. "Gwyndala left her post?"

Gwyn's voice spilled out of the badge. *"Dal. I'm sorry. I—"*

"We're in a warehouse. We came in through an alley. Find us."

"Dal, I—"

"I can't talk anymore. They've got us tied up, and I can't let them know we have a combadge." Dal squeezed the badge in his fist and looked up at the others.

"What are we going to do?" Rok-Tahk asked, and Dal didn't have an answer.

CHAPTER SEVEN

"**M**urf! What are we going to do?"

Gwyn was sitting at a rickety table beside a stand selling Romulan street food, a carton of noodles sitting in front of her. The owner was Romulan himself, and when she'd wandered by and smelled the delicious, fried-oil scent of Romulan noodles, she tried the same trick of speaking to the owner in his native tongue to sweet-talk him into giving her some. It had worked, but she'd only had a chance to eat one piece of the crispy deliciousness before Dal had contacted her on the combadge.

Murf's response was to reach over and eat her noodles in one big bite. Probably for the best—now she was too worried about the *Protostar*, and about her friends, to have much of an appetite.

"I wonder if I can make it back to the ship in time." Gwyn frowned. Murf made a concerned little gurgle, and she looked over at him.

"I wish my translator would translate you," she said with a wry smile.

Murf trilled and then slid off his chair and began rummaging around on the ground.

"I should call Janeway," Gwyn said, sitting up straight. But before she could tap her combadge, something soft bumped her leg. She looked down to find Murf gazing up at her, his lower body wrapped around her ankle. As she watched, he unwound it, then wound it around again and met her gaze.

"Dal!" she said. "You're right! He said they were tied up!"

Murf squeaked excitedly, then repeated the motion, wrapping and unwrapping himself around her ankle.

"You think we should go save Dal!" Gwyn said, wide-eyed.

Murf made a gurgling noise of agreement.

"Okay," she said. "But let's see what Janeway thinks too."

Murf nodded, and Gwyn tapped her combadge. "Janeway?"

Janeway's voice came through a second later. "*Janeway here.*"

"We have a problem," Gwyn said quickly, then told Janeway everything that Dal had told her. "Would it be better for me to come back to the ship or try to rescue the others? Murf thinks I should get the others."

"*I have to agree with Murf,*" Janeway said. "*As for the ship, I feel confident that the shields can handle whatever a gang of traders might throw at them.*"

"Are you sure?" Gwyn rapped her fingers nervously against the table. "I'll be as fast as I can, but I'm going to have to figure out where they are trapped."

"*These shields are designed to withstand heavy phaser cannon fire,*" Janeway said. "*And I'm equipped to protect the ship if need be. But I do think you getting your crewmates out of danger is imperative right now.*"

Gwyn nodded. "Okay. Sounds good. We'll let you know when we're on our way." She let out a deep breath. "You heard Janeway," she said to Murf. "We need to find the others as quickly as possible."

Murf blinked expectantly.

"Except Dal didn't tell me where they are." Gwyn drummed her fingers on the table. "And this whole place is full of traders. They could be anywhere in the market. Which is *huge*."

Murf made a low, sorrowful noise.

Gwyn fingered her communicator badge. Dal had told her that they were in a warehouse, which narrowed the location down somewhat—they were in a building somewhere.

"They came down through an alley," Gwyn murmured to Murf. "But there are tons of alleys around here!" She sighed and put her head in her hands. It would be so easy to hail Dal on the combadge—but if she did it at the wrong time, it could put Dal and the others in danger.

"I've got to figure this out," she whispered, staring down at the badge gleaming in her palm. What else had Dal told her? That there were traders coming for the *Protostar*—which meant they'd somehow known about the ship.

"They'd have equipment!" she said, sitting up in her chair. Murf looked at her quizzically.

"Dal said they were trapped by traders who wanted to strip the *Protostar* because they saw its energy signature. But that means they had to have the equipment to monitor for the signature! That should narrow things down quite a bit."

Murf jiggled in place, gurgling excitedly.

Gwyn stood up, pocketing her combadge. "We'll start with the Bajoran we met," she said. "She might know where we can go."

And then Gwyn and Murf stepped back out into the crowd.

▲

Dal sat back on his heels, staring at the key to the cage. It dangled from the closest wall, and he was trying to measure the distance with his eyes. He *might* be able to reach it, if he ever had a moment without Teyless or her crew nearby. If not, one of the long, thin arms on Zero's containment suit could do the trick. But until they were alone in the warehouse, Dal didn't want to risk untying anyone else.

"Ioma!" Teyless barked. She and her crew had been gathered around one of the crates on the far side of the warehouse, although Dal hadn't been able to see what they were up to. Now she peeled off away from the others and strolled in the direction of the cage.

"She's coming back!" Rok-Tahk hissed, scooting backward. Zero and Jankom shifted, drawing themselves up. Dal's muscles tensed.

Teyless stopped a few paces away, waiting for Ioma to catch up, his black coat fluttering out behind him. "Watch them," she said in a sharp voice.

"What?" Ioma's eyes shuddered sideways, a blink of surprise. "You said I could go on the next mission."

"Yeah, you did. You got them here." Teyless grinned and slapped Ioma on the shoulder. "Don't let them try anything funny."

"By 'next mission,' I didn't mean knocking into the big case-carrier there!" Ioma let out a hiss of disbelief. "I want to scavenge!"

"Sorry. Maybe next time." Teyless shrugged, then turned to the cage. "You four behave yourselves," she said cheerily. "Ioma will be here in case you need anything."

"How about you let us out?" Jankom shouted. He whirled around so he could punch at the cage with his multi-mitt. The bars rattled.

"Not until we've gotten what we need," Teyless said to him. Then she turned back to Ioma. "I'm serious. If they escape, it'll be your head."

"They're a bunch of kids," Ioma muttered. "You didn't even give me challenging prisoners."

"Oh, stop whining. You'll still get your cut." Teyless pushed past him and called out to the others. "Come on, let's get going! This ship isn't going to strip itself!"

Dal watched with a slow-growing horror as Teyless's crew fanned out from the crate, revealing what they'd been doing: preparing a massive, portable shield deflector.

"No!" cried Rok-Tahk, throwing herself up against the cage. Jankom rattled the bars harder. Zero just let out a dejected sigh.

"See?" Teyless said to Ioma. "You'll have your hands full."

Ioma scowled, watching as Teyless and the others shouldered their bags and filed out of the warehouse.

Dal was watching too, his heart thundering with hope. If they played their cards right, they might be able to get out of this yet.

He kicked at Jankom, who looked down at him in surprise. "The *Protostar*!" Jankom said. "They're going to—"

"I *know*," Dal said. Then he mouthed, *I have a plan*. This wasn't exactly true, but nothing was going to get done with Jankom rattling the cages.

"I can't believe this," Ioma muttered, shuffling over to Teyless's desk. Dal breathed. If they kept their voices down, they'd be able to talk.

"Dal?" Rok-Tahk turned around. "What are we going to do?"

"Sit down," Dal said softly. "Get close."

Rok-Tahk exchanged glances with Zero, who was the first to drift down close to Dal. "What are you thinking?" they whispered, glancing over their shoulder at Ioma.

"Don't look at him," Dal said. "We need him to forget that we're here."

Rok-Tahk frowned. "I don't think that's going to happen."

"Jankom Pog agrees! We need to act."

But Dal shook his head. "We need him to stop dwelling on us. To get distracted. Then I can untie all of you. *Then*"—Dal tilted his head toward the key—"maybe we can get ahold of that. Or try something else."

The others glanced at one another. Dal looked

past them to where Ioma had kicked back with his feet on Teyless's desk.

Oh, Dal thought, *this is going to be easy.*

"He's barely paying attention to us now," Dal said. "Let's give it a little bit more time. We can talk quietly. Figure out what we're going to do once we're untied."

"What about Gwyn?" Rok-Tahk said. "Can we contact her again? At least let her know where we are."

Dal frowned. "I don't think we should risk it. If he hears her voice, he's going to take the combadge away. Which means he'll get close enough to—"

"To see your hands are untied," Zero finished. "Yes, I agree. Better to try to escape ourselves."

Rok-Tahk nodded, although she was still worried about Gwyn—and about Murf, who Gwyn had said was with her. What if Murf ate something expensive and got caught? Gwyn wouldn't be able to rescue him *and* the crew—would she?

"So what are we going to do once you get our hands untied?" Jankom asked.

"The key." Dal nodded with his chin. "One of us should be able to reach out to grab it."

But Jankom only let out a hearty laugh. "No. Too far."

Dal frowned. "I don't think so. I bet I could reach. Or Zero."

"Oh, no, I don't think I could reach," Zero said. "My arms simply aren't long enough."

"Yeah, but you're noncorporeal," Dal said. "Just let yourself out of that containment suit and drift over there."

"No!" Zero cried. "How could you even suggest that! You know what happens if someone sees me outside of my containment suit!"

The crew fell quiet—they did all know. Because Zero was a Medusan, seeing Zero's form outside of their containment suit was enough to drive someone mad. The Diviner had used Zero as a weapon. As a thing. And Zero was still recovering from those memories.

"Rok-Tahk?" Dal said, quickly changing the subject. "Do you think you could reach?"

"I can't even fit my arm through the bars!" Rok-Tahk cried.

Dal threw his hands up in frustration—then quickly tucked them behind his back. Fortunately,

Ioma was tapping on a PADD over at Teyless's desk, not paying any attention to them.

"If you hadn't lost the battery," he said to Rok-Tahk, "we wouldn't even be in this situation."

Rok-Tahk's eyes narrowed in anger. "Excuse me? You're blaming *me*? They didn't even want the battery. They just wanted the *Protostar*."

"Yeah, but this all could have played out differently if you hadn't lost the battery!" Dal cried.

"Well, you shouldn't have told me I had to carry it, then," Rok-Tahk snapped. "You're no better than Jankom, making me play at being his bodyguard!"

"Hey, what'd Jankom Pog do?" Jankom frowned. "Jankom Pog thought we were having fun!"

"No!" Rok-Tahk shouted. "*You* were having fun. I had to act all big and scary just because of how I look!" She slumped down against the cage. "I didn't want to take the battery, but Dal made me. Because I *look* like I should be the security officer. But I've told you hundreds of times—"

"Will you kids knock it off over there?" Ioma's voice rang out through the warehouse. Rok-Tahk snapped her mouth shut, her eyes wide, and looked over at him. He was still sitting at the desk, tapping on his PADD. "You're disrupting my concentration," he added.

Rok-Tahk sighed. When she spoke again, she kept her voice low. "I just wish you'd listened when I said I didn't want to."

Dal frowned. Zero drifted over to Rok-Tahk and patted her shoulder softly. "I know how you feel," they said. "But I don't think Dal meant anything by it."

Rok-Tahk sniffled. "It would have been better for Dal to take it." She looked up at him, and he felt himself shrink a little under her gaze.

"Maybe you're right," he said. "I—"

But before Dal could finish, a bell chimed through the warehouse.

Ioma cursed and threw his PADD down on the desk. He looked over at Dal's crew, eyes flashing. The bell rang again. "I've got to take care of this," he said. "If you kids try anything—*anything*—it'll be your heads."

The crew looked at one another. Dal felt a stirring of hope. *Here's our chance,* he thought.

"Don't worry about us," Dal said with a smooth smile. "We'll be right here when you get back."

CHAPTER EIGHT

Gwyn pressed her hand against the doorbell again, listening to it echo through the building.

"This might be another dead end," she said to Murf, who gurgled in response.

She tried the door one more time—still locked. This was the third warehouse she tried after talking to the Bajoran woman. Gwyn hadn't told her the *whole* truth, of course. Just that her friends had met up with some traders at a warehouse, but she didn't have a way to contact them to ask where, exactly. Her new friend had happily given her a list of addresses.

"Be careful, though," the Bajoran had said, her ridged brow furrowed with concern. "Some of those places don't have the best reputation."

Gwyn rang the doorbell one more time for good measure. "All right, let's go," she said to Murf. "There's one more address on our list, and—"

Murf jumped up excitedly, and that was when Gwyn heard it too. Footsteps on the other side.

She immediately straightened up and pulled off the heirloom fretwork she wore around her wrist. The fretwork was a gift from her father—the only thing, in fact, that he'd ever given her. As beautiful as it was, he'd only ever intended for her to use it as a weapon.

And if she was going to get inside that warehouse, she needed to offer something valuable to trade.

The door scraped open, and a slim, reptilian face peered out, his eyes narrowed in suspicion. "Yes," he said. "Can I help you?"

Gwyn tried to look past him, but he blocked the view with his body. She held up the fretwork. "I heard I could come to you if I needed chimerium."

"We're closed." The man started to drag the door shut, but Gwyn sent her fretwork shooting out to block it, the metal warping and solidifying over the course of a heartbeat. The door clanged as it slammed into the fretwork, which was now shaped more like a spear than a bracelet.

Her trick had the desired effect, as the trader's eyes went wide with excitement. He shoved the door open again. "How'd you do that?"

Gwyn pulled the fretwork back into a bracelet. She managed to catch a glimpse of the room beyond the door. It was small, closed off. There was no sign of Dal or the others.

"With my mind," she said.

"Mind-controlled metal?" The trader stepped forward, his hand reaching out to touch the heirloom. Gwyn pulled it away.

"It comes from the planet of Solum," she said, trying to keep her voice steady. "There's a race of people who live there. The Vau N'Akat. They—they're very isolated. They believe they're alone in the universe."

Her words were intriguing the trader, and he pushed the door open wider. "They made that?" he rasped, nodding at the heirloom.

Gwyn nodded.

"How'd you get it?"

Gwyn smiled sweetly. "It's a fascinating story. But I'll only tell it if you decide to buy."

The trader scratched his chin with a curved claw. "I might be able to make a deal. My name's Ioma. Why don't you come in?"

He stepped back, and Gwyn and Murf entered the small, dark room. It was empty, but there was another door in the back wall.

"This way," Ioma said, leading her over to the door. Gwyn held her breath, her fingers curled tightly around the heirloom. *Please let them be here.*

He swung the door open and went through. Gwyn followed him into a cavernous warehouse. Her eyes swept around. A small transporter pad. Stacks and stacks of crates. A messy desk. And—

Murf yelped in excitement and began slithering toward the big cage on the very far side of the warehouse. Toward Dal and Jankom and Zero and Rok-Tahk, all of them locked inside, their hands tied behind their backs.

"Not so fast, buddy." Ioma slammed his foot in front of Murf, blocking his path. "You two can wait over at the desk."

"Who—who are those people?" Gwyn said, trying to keep her voice level. "In the cage?"

"Thieves," Ioma said without missing a beat. "Got

caught stealing from Teyless. She's the boss around here."

"So she's the one I need to talk to about selling my heirloom," Gwyn said.

Ioma grinned at her, showing a row of spiky teeth. "Well, no. 'Cause she ain't here right now. So I guess it'll be the two of us having a conversation, won't it?"

Gwyn forced herself to look at the trader and not at her friends locked away in the cage. Murf gurgled at her feet.

"I guess it will," she said sweetly. "Assuming you have something to trade for it."

Ioma laughed and swept his arm out wide. "I've got everything you see here in the warehouse."

Gwyn raised an eyebrow. "Including those folks in the cage? I could use some good workers—"

"Ah, no." Ioma shook his head wildly, fear flashing in his eyes. "Ain't no slaver."

It was worth a shot, Gwyn thought. "Well, I'm sure we can reach some kind of agreement."

Ioma regained his composure and gestured toward a messy desk set up in the corner. "Let's talk."

He turned and loped toward the desk. Gwyn

followed him, shooting one last glance back at the crew. Dal waved at her. His hands were untied! Good to know. She nodded her acknowledgment.

"Let me see that bracelet again," Ioma said as he slid into the chair behind the desk. Gwyn unhooked the heirloom and set it down on the center of the table, although she kept her hand on it, pinning it in place.

"Happy to oblige," she said, "but I'm going to need some kind of collateral."

Ioma looked at her, yellow eyes glittering. She stared right back.

"Fine," he said, reaching into his coat. He pulled out a shiny silver phaser and set it on the desk. "Just to show you how trusting I am," he said. "If I try any funny business, you can stun me as I stand." He gestured at himself, even though he was sitting.

Gwyn was shocked at how lucky she'd gotten. "Fair enough," she said, wrapping her hand around the grip of the phaser at the same time that she released her heirloom. Ioma snatched it up, frowning down at it. Gwyn slid the phaser closer to her.

"This thing's mind controlled, you said?" He turned it over in his hand.

"Sure is." Gwyn glanced down at Murf, then jerked her head back toward the cage. Murf nodded, then slipped away, moving silently across the cold floor.

Gwyn leaned forward over the desk. "Do you want me to show you how it works?"

"Of course I do!" Ioma's head snapped up; for a moment, Gwyn froze, certain he would see Murf. But he only tossed the heirloom at her. "Because right now it just looks like a bracelet."

"You saw what it could do earlier." Gwyn smiled. Then she concentrated, and the metal of the heirloom grew malleable, flattening out into a large, sturdy disk. "It's not just a weapon," she said, picking it up and sliding the new form onto her arm. "It can be used as a shield." She concentrated again, and the heirloom re-formed into a long curved dagger. "Or a knife. Or whatever you need."

"Yes, but how could *I* do that?" Ioma demanded. "It's useless if you're the only one who can control it."

"I'll show you." Gwyn's heart pounded in her chest. In truth, only a Vau N'Akat had the capacity to control the matter that comprised the heirloom, and even then, it took years of working with a particular piece to be able to control it well. But she was reasonably sure she could fake it in the time it took Murf to get her friends out of the cage.

Because if anyone could break the crew out of that cage, it was Murf.

"Okay, then." Ioma straightened up. "That's what I wanted."

Gwyn reshaped the heirloom back into a bracelet and handed it to him. He tried to slide it onto his wrist, but it was too small. "I can't even—"

In her mind, Gwyn enlarged the bracelet slightly, and it slipped perfectly onto the trader's arm.

He hissed something in a language her translator couldn't pick up, bouncing excitedly in his chair. "I did that!" he cried. "Didn't I? I wanted it to be bigger, and it was!"

"You're a natural." Gwyn risked glancing over her shoulder. Murf was at the cage, doing . . . something. She whipped her gaze back before Ioma realized what she was looking at. "Now, see if you can make it into a dagger."

The trader nodded excitedly, then stared down at the heirloom, his brow furrowed in concentration.

With his gaze off her, Gwyn glanced back at the cage again—

To see that the door was open! Somehow, Murf had done it, and it looked like Dal was in the process of untying the others' hands.

"Nothing's happening," Ioma whined.

Gwyn immediately turned back to him. She made the heirloom ripple.

"Wait! Did it—"

Gwyn made it ripple again.

"It did! I think something's working!" Ioma looked at her triumphantly—

And then his triumphant expression promptly twisted into one of rage.

"No, no, no, no!" he shouted, leaping to his feet. "How did you get that door open?"

The heirloom clattered to the desk, and Gwyn immediately turned it into a long thin staff, the material sliding neatly into her hand. She whipped the heirloom up, hitting Ioma in the stomach. He staggered backward, howling and cursing.

"Run!" she screamed at the crew as she jumped to her feet, grabbing Ioma's phaser with her free hand. She whirled around and dived across the floor, with Ioma's angry shouts following her.

"I'm still untying Jankom!" Dal shouted. "The rest of you, go!"

Rok-Tahk and Zero surged forward, their hands free. As she ran, Rok-Tahk bent down to scoop up Murf. Gwyn saw the glint of a key for just a second before it disappeared into the maw of Murf's mouth.

"This way," she said breathlessly, herding them toward the door.

"Stop!" Ioma roared. He jumped and landed in front of them, his mouth curled up in a snarl. "Back into the cage. All of you."

Gwyn lifted his phaser. It was set to stun, which meant it would only knock him out. But that would give them the time to escape—

He hit her hand, sent the phaser skittering across the floor. "I don't think so."

So Gwyn whacked him hard with her staff. He fell sideways, and she bolted forward. Rok-Tahk was right in front of her. Zero was off to her side, near a cluster of crates. "Dal!" she screamed, glancing back at him. To her relief, he and Jankom were racing across the warehouse.

"Right behind you!" Dal shouted.

Ioma moaned, pushing himself up.

"Watch out!" Zero called out. "He has a phas—"

A blast of light slammed through the air.

"He's shooting at us!" Jankom wailed.

"I'll hold him off!" Gwyn whirled around, her heirloom flowering out into a broad, flat shield just in time to block Ioma's phaser fire. Gwyn stumbled backward, then glanced over her shoulder: Rok-Tahk, Murf, and Zero had just ducked into the entrance door.

"Get back here!" Ioma shouted, moving toward the door. Gwyn reshaped the heirloom back into a staff and tripped him, sending him sprawling across the cold floor.

"Great shot!" Dal shouted as he zipped past her. Jankom was right behind him. "Get outside!"

Ioma was scrambling to his feet, his phaser still clutched in one hand. He fired two bolts in Jankom and Dal's direction, but Gwyn deflected them with her heirloom. She flattened it out into a shield that she held aloft as she jogged backward toward the door.

"Come on, come on!" Dal yelled.

"You kids really think you can get away from

me?" Ioma roared, shooting off bolts of phaser fire in Gwyn's direction. Fortunately, she felt herself spill through the doorway. Dal slammed the door shut and shoved a chair up against the knob. The whole thing rattled, Ioma pounding on the other side.

"Got him." Dal grinned.

The rattling stopped; footsteps faded on the other side of the door.

"He's definitely going out some other door," Gwyn said. "We need to get out of here *now*."

Dal nodded in agreement, and the two of them darted out into the alley, where the rest of the crew was waiting.

"You found us!" Rok-Tahk cried, throwing her arms around Gwyn's shoulder and squeezing her in tight.

"Yeah, I did," Gwyn said breathlessly. "But now we've got to get—"

A beam of light sliced overhead and hit the wall of the building, sending debris flying down onto the crew. Dal whirled around to find Ioma standing in the entrance of the alley, his phaser held high.

"Like I said." He smirked as he strolled forward toward the crew, who fell silent and pressed in close together at the sight of him. "You aren't going to get away from me."

He lifted his phaser, pointed it—

And let out a howl of surprise as Murf clamped his mouth over Ioma's free hand.

"Murf to the rescue again," Dal said. "Everybody! This way!" He tilted his head toward the opposite end of the alley, which opened into another part of the market.

"You go ahead," Gwyn said, fashioning her heirloom into a staff again before racing over to Ioma, whose hand was still stuck in Murf's mouth.

"Let go of me," he snarled through gritted teeth, lifting his phaser.

Gwyn slammed her staff into the side of his head, knocking him back. His hand slipped free of Murf's mouth, his fingers coated in glistening saliva.

"Good thinking," Gwyn said, scooping Murf up in her arms. "But it's time to go."

She took off down the alley, hunching over and weaving back and forth to avoid the fire from Ioma's phaser. As she rounded the corner, she found the others waiting for her. She handed Murf to Rok-Tahk, and together they took off running into the crowded market street.

Suddenly, screams erupted into the air. Gwyn glanced backward to see Ioma loping toward them. People scurried away from him, eyes wide at the sight of his phaser.

"He's back on us!" she shouted, ducking around a vendor's table piled high with shining ceramic bowls.

"That guy does not quit, does he?" Dal glanced backward at the parting crowd, Ioma surging toward them.

"We need a distraction." Zero whirred up beside them. "Something to get his eyes off us so we can escape."

Gwyn's eyes zipped around the market. It was flush with vendors and shoppers both, and she and the rest of the crew were barely managing to stay together as they wove their individual paths through the crush. And the constant shouts of fear and anger coming from behind them told her Ioma was hot on their tail.

Gwyn slammed into a thick knot of women wearing long silvery cloaks. She spun around, separated from the others. The women jostled her, shouting in annoyance. "I'm sorry," she said. "Excuse me, I just need to—"

"Got you." It was Zero, who flew down into the middle of the women. They grabbed Gwyn's hand and helped pull her free of the tangle and back into the street proper. "The others are up ahead," Zero said. "I think Jankom—"

But Zero couldn't finish their thought. A loud clatter exploded from farther up the street, and then something shot straight into the air. The crowd gasped and tilted their heads back.

"There's Jankom's distraction," Zero said cheerfully. "Come on."

"What's he going to do?" Gwyn tilted her head upward as Zero led her through the crowd.

Zero didn't have to answer, because the object exploded overhead into a brilliant burst of light and glitter. Gwyn let out a laugh.

"It seems Jankom found himself a firework," Zero said, sounding amused.

The light was still shimmering overhead, and the crowd began applauding. Through the clamor, Gwyn caught sight of Rok-Tahk, who was holding on tight to Murf as she scanned the crowd.

"There they are!" Rok-Tahk shouted to Dal and Jankom. She pointed across the crowd to where Gwyn was waving excitedly as she ran forward. But Zero—

"Where'd Zero go?" Panic seized at Rok-Tahk's chest.

"That light display isn't going to last much longer," Jankom said. "And Jankom only has one more."

Gwyn rushed up to them. "Let's go," she said.

"Zero fell behind." Dal surged forward, his eyes searching—

Then he saw it, a faint glint of metal. Zero came up out of the crowd, then slammed back down.

"Is it that reptilian trader? It looks like someone grabbed Zero." Gwyn felt her heirloom ripple against her arm in anticipation.

Jankom's light show twinkled, the lights swirling together into the shape of a Klingon ship called a Bird-of-Prey, which zoomed and darted through the air, much to the delight of the crowd.

"It's those women!" Rok-Tahk cried. "In the silvery cloaks! They've got Zero!"

As soon as Rok-Tahk spoke, Gwyn saw it too—the women separated for a moment to reveal that two of them held Zero firmly in place.

"Everyone? Ioma is close." Rok-Tahk's fearful voice interrupted Gwyn's thoughts. She whipped her head over and saw him speaking to a Ferengi vendor. To her great relief, the vendor shook his head.

"I think he's asking people if they've seen us. Let's grab Zero and get out of here," Gwyn said.

"Good call," Dal said. "Rok-Tahk, Jankom. Let's go."

The last of the light show twinkled away, and the crowd was returning to their slow milling around. Dal darted forward, aware of the others behind him. The silver-cloaked women murmured over Zero, who struggled against their grip.

"Let me go!" they cried. "I'm not—"

"Could fetch a pretty penny," one of the women said just as Dal popped his head up between them.

"Not for sale," Dal said with a grin.

Just as he'd hoped, his appearance was enough to startle them into loosening their grip on Zero, who zipped straight up, out of harm's way.

"See ya," Dal added before sliding back out into the crowd, rejoining Gwyn, Rok-Tahk, and Jankom.

"Thank you," Zero said, the light in their display swirling softly. "I was afraid—"

"We'll never leave a crew member behind," Rok-Tahk said, hugging Murf close.

"All right, Jankom." Dal grinned. "Time for the grand finale."

Jankom nodded, then pulled the second firework out of his pocket. He activated the cord with his multi-mitt.

A heartbeat later, light exploded over the market, and the *Protostar* crew made their escape.

CHAPTER NINE

The ground vehicle zoomed through the trees, heading in the direction of the *Protostar*. Dal was driving, his fingers poised over the controls as he zoomed down the path.

"Um, maybe slow down?" Jankom clung to the side of the vehicle, his eyes wide. "You almost hit that—ahh!"

Dal wrenched the vehicle away from a low-hanging tree branch at the last minute, sending everyone in the vehicle careening off to one side and setting off a chorus of protests.

"Sorry," Dal said, whipping the vehicle in the other direction. "But Teyless and her scavenging crew could be stripping our ship as we speak!" He glanced at Jankom. "At least I have a reason for driving like a maniac."

"I did leave the deflector shields up!" Gwyn shouted from the backseat.

"They have a way of getting through those!" The vehicle's console map beeped. Dal glanced down to see they were approaching the *Protostar*'s location. He slowed down.

"Oh, thank goodness," Zero said. "I was afraid I was going to get flung out the back window."

"Hey, I got us here in record time." Dal grinned and drew up on the controls, holographic lights fluttering around his fingers. Slowly, the vehicle came to a stop near a particularly wide tree.

"Where's the ship?" Rok-Tahk asked, worry in her voice.

"Just up ahead. We'll walk the rest of the way so the traders don't hear our vehicle." Dal shut off the vehicle's power and jumped out, landing softly on the spongy forest floor. He tilted his head, listening; it was quiet out here among the trees, save for the rushing of the wind in the branches, the babble of the nearby river, and—

Voices.

"I hear them," Gwyn said softly, stepping up alongside Dal.

Dal nodded. The voices of the traders came drifting faintly through the forest. He couldn't make out exactly what they were saying, but they sounded excited.

Suddenly, the quiet was shattered by a loud, grinding whine. Jankom surged forward, his movement frantic.

"The shields!" he cried. "That sound is the shields failing."

Dal caught Jankom before he ran up any closer to the ship. "Failing," he said into Jankom's ear. "But not totally depleted, right?"

Jankom nodded, listening to the loud whine. "Yes," he said. "But it's close."

"How close?" Gwyn asked.

Jankom shook his head. "Can't tell from listening. Jankom Pog would need to see the shields to know for sure."

Dal nodded. "Then we'll get closer. See how much time we have."

He glanced back to the crew's worried faces. "How are we going to get aboard?" Rok-Tahk said sadly. "We still can't use the transporters safely!"

"Once we know how much time we have, we'll

figure something out." Dal flashed her a smile that looked braver than he felt. "I promise."

The crew crept forward through the trees. It wasn't long before Dal saw dots of light glinting through the cool, shadowy green of the forest— the sun bouncing off the *Protostar*'s hull. He pulled Jankom alongside him, putting a finger to his lips.

"What do you want Jankom—"

"Be quiet!" Dal hissed. "We're almost there."

They crawled through the underbrush, branches snapping around them. Fortunately, the whining of Teyless's mobile shield deflector masked most of the noise.

Dal paused right at the edge of the underbrush. Through the tangle of greenery, he could see the *Protostar* next to the river, gleaming and unharmed. It was wrapped in a pale white glow—the shields.

As Dal watched, the shields flickered once.

"We're almost there!" Teyless shouted triumphantly. She looked up from the shield deflector and squinted at the ship. "I think ten more minutes should do the trick."

Dal's chest tightened. He glanced over at

Jankom, who was staring out at the ship with huge, frightened eyes.

"Jankom Pog thinks it'll be even less than that," he whispered sadly.

Dal stared at the *Protostar*. He and the others had fought so hard for it—the *Protostar* had been the reason they escaped from Tars Lamora in the first place. Then it had become their home among the stars, allowing them to see worlds none of them could ever have dreamed of when they were trapped working under the Diviner's cold rule.

And now they were about to lose all of it to a gang of traders from some backwater thieves' market.

"Come on," Dal whispered. "Let's go back to the others."

Jankom looked over at Dal in horror. "But the shields!" he cried. "If we don't do something, Teyless is going to get through!"

As he spoke, the shields flickered again. Teyless, Chadossa, and T'agross all let out a round of excited whoops.

"Which is why we're going to do something," Dal said with a smirk.

"We've got five minutes until the shields are drained," Dal announced as he and Jankom strode into the clearing where the others were waiting.

"What?" cried Rok-Tahk. "Are you sure?"

"Very sure," Jankom said sadly.

"What are we going to do?" Gwyn said. "Do we want to try the transporters?"

"Nope." Dal grinned at them before slapping his hand down on his communicator badge. "Dal to Janeway."

Gwyn frowned and glanced questioningly over at Jankom.

"He didn't tell Jankom Pog what he was up to."

"He's up to something?" Zero asked.

"*This is Janeway.*" Her familiar voice came through Dal's combadge. "*I'm glad to hear from you. We have an issue.*"

"With the shields, I know. We're all right outside the ship."

"*Then you know who's doing this.*"

"It's some rogue traders. Listen . . ." Dal took a deep breath. "Lift the shields."

"What!"

"Are you serious?"

"Jankom Pog says that's a terrible idea!"

Dal held up one hand to silence his friends' protests. "Janeway. Lift the shields, then deflect all power to the vehicle replicator."

Janeway waited a beat before saying, *"Are you sure those are your orders?"*

"Positive. Dal out." He tapped his combadge and looked at the others, all of whom were utterly baffled by his decision.

"The vehicle replicator?" Jankom sputtered.

From the other side of the trees, the loud whining suddenly cut off. A second later, the traders erupted into victorious cheers.

"Come on, we need to get to the *Protostar* now. Before they board."

"Get over there?" Gwyn stepped forward, shock rippling through her. "You want to get captured again?"

Dal's grin widened. "I do."

"But *why*?" Gwyn shook her head. "I just rescued you from them!"

The voices of the traders carried through the trees: primarily Teyless barking orders at T'agross and Chadossa to get their gear together.

"This is different," Dal said. "This time, we're

getting captured *on purpose*."

This explanation was met with baffled silence.

"Is there any way you could explain further?" Zero asked, choosing, as they usually did, to stay out of Dal's thoughts. "What are you planning to do with the vehicle replicator, to begin with?"

Dal sighed in frustration. "Look. We need to surrender before they board the ship. Okay? Will you all just *trust* me?"

For a moment, no one moved. Then Gwyn stepped forward.

"Fine," she said. "I'll see where this is going."

"Thank you." Dal grinned. "We're not going to get thrown into another cage. I promise."

Rok-Tahk and Zero looked at each other. Rok-Tahk looked down at Murf, who nodded his head.

"As long as I don't have to be anyone's bodyguard," Rok-Tahk sighed.

"You won't." Dal nodded. "Come on, Jankom."

"Sure. What else does Jankom Pog have to lose?" He threw his hands up. "Just the whole ship."

"We're not going to lose the ship." Dal turned away from the others and strode toward the *Protostar*. "I've got a plan."

A few moments later, Dal stepped out of the tree line and along the riverbank, where the *Protostar* was waiting. Teyless stood with her arms crossed over her chest as T'agross argued with Chadossa over who got to carry the pulse rifle.

"No one's on that ship," Teyless said with a sigh. "Could you two just—"

"Hey!" Dal shouted.

Teyless froze, then turned toward Dal. When she saw him—and the rest of the crew—she let out a string of words the translator didn't see fit to translate. All Dal heard was, "Ugh, Ioma!"

"I wanted to make a deal," Dal said. "A real one."

Teyless smirked, her lip curling up around her tusks. "Will you be attempting to trade a bag full of rocks again?"

Rok-Tahk glared at Teyless. Teyless only chuckled, then began striding toward the crew. Dal could sense his crewmates tensing up behind him.

"Teyless, what are you doing?" T'agross shouted. "These kids aren't going to do anything, even if they aren't locked up."

Teyless held up one hand, and the Klingon fell

silent. She narrowed her eyes at Dal. "He has a point," she said. "We broke through your shields. You have no weapons, and I have one of the greatest fighters on Odaru helping me out. I'm not sure what you think you're accomplishing here."

Dal lifted his chin defiantly. "I told you, we're here to make a deal. We surrender."

"You surrender?" Teyless let out a burst of laughter. "You managed to get away from Ioma— who is, admittedly, *not* one of the best fighters on Odaru, just so you can come here and surrender?"

Dal felt his chest tighten. He hadn't expected her to protest.

But then Gwyn stepped forward. "I rescued them," she said.

Teyless nodded with something that almost looked like approval.

"But we realized, after we got away—" Gwyn took a deep breath, glanced sideways at Dal. She only hoped she'd bought him enough time to come up with an excuse.

"That we need our ship more than we need anything else." The words came out of Dal's mouth in a rush. "And we've got some top-notch treasures on board. Stuff like—"

"Like this." Gwyn let her heirloom unwrap from her arm. And just as it had captured Ioma's fancy instantly, it also caught Teyless's.

"What *is* that?" she breathed.

"Just something we found on our travels." Gwyn let the heirloom settle back into a bracelet. "I've got others. If you take us aboard the ship, I'll show you where I store them."

"Not to mention the chimerium," Dal added quickly. "You'd be surprised what a group of *kids* can make off with."

Teyless cocked her head. "You have chimerium?"

Dal nodded. He was distantly aware of Rok-Tahk wrapping her arm around Jankom's mouth to keep him from shouting something about how they did not, in fact, have any chimerium. He made a mental note to thank her later.

"So why were you trying to trade a battery?" Teyless asked, her eyes narrowed. "Why not just buy what you needed?"

Dal crossed his arms over his chest. "Well, we assumed it'd be safer to trade the battery rather than cart around the amount of chimerium we'd

need. We were wrong, but hey? What can you do?"
He grinned.

Teyless studied him for a long time, then flicked
her gaze behind him, to Rok-Tahk and Gwyn and
and Murf and Jankom and Zero. Dal held his breath,
his heart pounding.

"Teyless?" Chadossa called out. "Are we boarding
or not?"

"We are," Teyless called back. "But we have a new
plan. No more stripping the ship." She smiled down
at Dal, showing all her teeth. "We're going treasure
hunting instead."

CHAPTER TEN

Zero floated behind Rok-Tahk, still uncertain what exactly Dal had in mind. Why had he told Teyless they had chimerium aboard the ship? And what was Teyless going to say when she found out that it was all a lie? They glanced over at Dal, trying to decide if they should dip into his thoughts or not.

"All right, kids. Stay close. No sudden moves." Teyless marched up the ramp and into the storage bay of the *Protostar*. T'agross and Chadossa rounded up Zero and the others, leading them in behind her. Zero wobbled nervously as they floated onboard.

"So where's this chimerium?" Teyless demanded, whirling around to face the nervous crew. Only Dal seemed confident.

"Locked away in a safe."

"Then open it," she snapped.

"Sure thing." Dal strolled up to her, then stopped, lifting one finger as if he'd just remembered something. "Oh. Wait a minute."

Teyless sighed. "What is it now?" She leaned down to him, her eyes glinting. "Did you suddenly remember that you spent all your chimerium? That this whole thing was a big lie?" She bared her tusks.

Dal chuckled, taking a step back from her. "Of course not! But Zero's going to need to go up into the ship's ducts to activate the antilock on the safe."

Teyless blinked, straightened up. "Which one of you is Zero?"

"Um, I am." Zero flitted forward, hoping that they didn't come across as frightened. As they did, Dal caught their eye and nodded once, very shortly, and Zero understood instantly: Dal was giving them permission to peek in his head and see his plan.

"Oh." Teyless studied them. "Let me guess. You're the only one who can fit in the ship's ducts?"

"Y-yes, I'm afraid so." Zero tried to infuse their voice with the same confidence that Dal spoke with. "It's a protective measure. You understand."

As they spoke, Zero let their own thoughts wander

over to Dal's. Dal's plan came to Zero in a series of images: Zero going to the vehicle replicator rather than the ducts. Zero replicating a pile of chimerium, then setting it inside a clear wall panel within one of the escape pods. Instantly, Zero understood exactly what Dal hoped would happen.

"Fine," Teyless said. "But if I get a whiff of anything amiss—and I mean *anything*, I won't hesitate to kill your friends, one by one."

Rok-Tahk let out a frightened gasp. Jankom started to protest. "You wouldn't—"

Gwyn cut him off, slapping her hand over his mouth.

"Understood," Zero said, hearing their confidence edge out their fear.

Teyless flicked her wrist dismissively. As Zero flew out of the storage bay and into the corridor of the ship, they heard T'agross barking at the crew to sit down against the wall.

I just hope this plan works out the way Dal expects it to, thought Zero.

They flew as quickly as they could down the corridor, trying very hard not to think about Teyless's threat to kill their friends one by one.

Fortunately, they arrived at the vehicle replicator without any interruption. The replicator hummed with power. Zero moved over to the control panel. "Replicate chimerium," they said, then paused, sick with worry.

"Chimerium cannot be replicated," the computer said.

Terror ripped through Zero. They thought of the crew lined up against the wall—Gwyn and Dal would be putting on an air of confidence, certainly. Probably Jankom, too. But Rok-Tahk would be terrified.

"I know that," Zero said quickly. "I mean, replicate a substance that looks like chimerium?"

The replicator paused for a moment. "Do you wish to replicate false chimerium?"

"Yes!" Zero cried. "False chimerium. It just has to look good."

"Understood."

Then, to Zero's great relief, the replicator lit up, and a small pile of chimerium—false chimerium—appeared on the platform. To Zero, it looked like the real thing, glittering in the bright lights of the room. Perhaps Teyless wouldn't be able to tell the difference until she and her crew were off the ship.

Zero scooped up the false chimerium and tucked it away in one of the escape pods, just as Dal had planned.

▲

"Your Medusan friend is taking too long," Teyless said to Dal.

"They just left!" Dal cried.

Teyless huffed her displeasure, then nodded at Chadossa. The Caitian immediately snatched Murf out of Rok-Tahk's arms.

"Hey!" Rok-Tahk shouted. "What are you doing? Leave him alone!"

Murf squirmed against Chadossa's embrace. "Oh, disgusting. It's all slimy," she hissed.

"Don't say that about Murf!" Rok-Tahk snapped.

"He is kind of slimy," Jankom muttered.

Rok-Tahk smacked Jankom on the arm.

"No sudden movements!" T'agross roared, pointing a pulse rifle at them. Rok-Tahk went still, her eyes wide.

Teyless turned to Dal. "If the Medusan is not back in five—"

"All done!"

Dal let out a long sigh of relief as Zero zoomed back

into the storage bay. Teyless turned toward them.

"You've activated the antilock device?" she said with a sneer.

"I did," Zero said pleasantly. "Although only on the first safe on the right."

They glanced over at Dal, who nodded. Of course, that had been the escape pod Zero had seen in Dal's mind, but they didn't want to take any chances.

"Well, I hope you unlocked the one with the chimerium," Teyless snapped.

"Of course," Zero said. "Why wouldn't I?"

Teyless grunted in annoyance. "All right, everyone!" She clapped her hands together, whirling around to face the crew. "We're going on a little expedition. Line up single file."

The crew glanced nervously at one another. Gwyn was the first to stand up.

"Come on," she said with a smile. "Everything will be fine."

Zero went over to Gwyn's side, settling in place behind her. When Dal walked over to join them, Teyless grabbed his arm and pulled him roughly to her side.

"Not you," she said. "You're coming with me."

Dal smiled past his thundering heart. Teyless shoved him forward, marching him over to the exit. Dal stiffened when he felt the tip of her phaser stick into his back.

"Take us to the safes," she said. "And don't try anything funny."

Dal looked up at her. "Have we done anything funny since we got here?"

Teyless had no answer.

Dal glanced over his shoulder to check on the others: to his relief, they were being marched along by both T'agross and Chadossa. Good. He needed all three traders to be in one place.

"Turn left," he said cheerfully as they approached the cross corridor. Teyless grunted in acknowledgment.

They walked down the corridor without speaking. Dal kept his stride loose and easy, trying not to betray the frantic rhythm of his heartbeat. Teyless, at least, seemed to buy it.

"How much farther?" she asked. "We're just winding down hallways."

"Almost there," Dal said. "We keep the safe in an, um, unusual location."

Teyless looked at him, tusks flashing. "I don't like unusual."

Dal grinned. "Look, we're a bunch of kids robbing starships. We've got to think creatively."

Her brow furrowed. "If this is a trap—"

"It's not a trap," Dal said quickly. "But we've had to abandon ship on more than one occasion. So we keep all our safes—"

He turned abruptly, pulling her into the escape pod room.

"Where we can take them with us if we have to."

Teyless's two associates dragged the others into the escape pod room. "Up against the wall," T'agross ordered. "And don't move." He turned to Teyless. "What's going on here? Why are we in the escape room?"

Dal held his breath.

But Teyless just broke into a smile. "These kids might deserve more credit than we've given them," she said. "Their 'captain' here tells me he keeps all their loot aboard an escape pod."

"Just like you do!" cried Chadossa. Teyless shot her a dirty look, and she immediately cowered, ears flat against her head.

"Hey, great minds," Dal said, nudging her.

"Enough from you. Which pod is it?"

"First pod on the right," Dal said. "There is, uh, a *tiny* complication, though."

Teyless whirled toward him, anger flashing across her features. "Complication? What sort of complication? I let your Medusan roam the corridors unsupervised—"

"It's nothing!" Dal said, peeling himself away from her. "Just an additional fail-safe to cut down on thievery."

Teyless arched an eyebrow.

"Got to have at least four people in the pod in order to open the safe," Dal said.

Teyless stared at him for a long time. Dal gestured back at his crew.

"Look, I love 'em," he said. "But there's six of us. So a majority has always got to be present—"

"I get it." Teyless waved her hand. "T'agross. Chadossa. Leave the kids and get over here."

"Are you sure?" T'agross frowned down at the crew. "They're rather—feisty."

"Yes, yes. I'm sure." Teyless sighed.

As T'agross and Chadossa stepped across the

room, Dal caught Gwyn's eye, then jerked his head, very slightly, in the direction of the escape pod's emergency release.

She nodded in understanding.

Dal spun around and strode up to the first escape pod on the right, activating the doors with one fluid motion. They hissed open, and Teyless let out an excited gasp.

The false chimerium that Zero had replicated was sitting in plain sight, tucked into a panel on the wall, an energy shield keeping it safe.

"Right this way," Dal said, bowing graciously.

"Look at that," Teyless said. "You kids weren't lying." Then she nodded at Chadossa, her voice going hard. "You first."

"Oh, I assure you, there's no trap," Dal said.

"I don't care what you say," Teyless snapped back. "Chadossa, get in there."

Her whiskers quivering, the Caitian stepped into the escape pod. When nothing happened, Teyless nodded at T'agross, who went in, peering around the space.

"That doesn't really look like a safe," he grumbled. "The chimerium just out in the open like that."

"Zero figured you'd want to see it," Dal said. He turned to Teyless, gestured expansively. "Ladies first."

"You are not as charming as you think you are," she said coldly as she stepped across the boundary.

"Oh, but I am." Dal winked at her—

And slammed his fist down on the door's control panel, locking all three of the traders inside.

"Now!" he shouted—which was completely unnecessary, because Gwyn was already activating the emergency release. The escape pod moaned as its safety grip sprung free. Dal stepped back, grinning.

Teyless's face appeared in the tiny view window, her expression twisted up in fury. But whatever she was screaming, Dal couldn't hear.

And then he couldn't see her either, as the escape pod flung itself up into Odaru's atmosphere, back to the market where it was programmed to land.

CHAPTER ELEVEN

*T*he *Protostar* burst through Odaru's atmosphere with a billow of oxygen and flame. But its entire crew was safely inside, tucked away on the ship's bridge, chattering excitedly to Janeway about everything that had just happened.

"The look on Teyless's face!" Jankom rolled around on the floor beside the second navigation station, roaring with laughter. "Priceless."

"It was a very clever plan." Janeway smiled. "Although I hope the six of you have learned how important it is to respect one another's wishes. It seems this whole thing could have been avoided if you'd done so."

"Even though it was super awesome?" Jankom interrupted.

"Even then." Janeway nodded toward him.

Dal settled back in the captain's seat, watching the stars blink on through the viewing screen. Rok-Tahk had lifted the ship out of Odaru's orbit, and now that they were free of its atmosphere, she turned back to him.

"Where to?" she said.

It was a simple question, and one that normally excited her. But Dal heard a glint of sadness there too. He frowned.

"We'll just cruise for a while," he said.

She nodded and turned back to her controls. Dal glanced over at Janeway.

It's important to respect one another's wishes.

Dal jumped up from his seat and swung down to Rok-Tahk's station. She looked up at him, surprise and confusion washing across her face.

"I wanted to apologize," he said.

Rok-Tahk blinked. Dal could sense the others turning their gaze toward the two of them. Which was fine. He'd like them all to hear what he had to say.

"I'm sorry I made you carry the replicated battery," he said. "You made it clear that you didn't want to, and I told you to do it anyway. I should have been the one to carry it."

Rok-Tahk stared at him, her eyes wide. "You mean it?" she whispered.

"Yeah." Dal smiled and draped his arm around her in a quick hug. "I know you don't like being used just for your muscle. It's like Janeway said. We've got to respect one another's wishes. I should have done that."

Rok-Tahk smiled at him. "Thanks, Dal."

"Jankom Pog's also sorry." Jankom sat up, looking over at Rok-Tahk. "He should not have asked you to be Fafnir Avant's bodyguard."

Rok-Tahk laughed a little. "Thanks, Jankom," she said. "Although I guess that part wasn't so bad. I'd just like to be someone else next time."

"Maybe you can be Fafnir Avant's scientist friend," Jankom said. "Every rogue trader's got to have one, right?"

"Not really, no," Dal said, only to be smacked on the arm by Gwyn.

"I think that's an excellent idea, Jankom," she said.

Jankom beamed at her.

Dal patted Rok-Tahk on the shoulder, then turned to Zero, who was resting near the communication wall. As Gwyn, Jankom, and Rok-Tahk began spinning out a story about Fafnir Avant's next exploits, Dal made his way over to Zero, then sat down beside them.

"Thanks for replicating that fake chimerium," Dal said. "I hope looking in on my thoughts wasn't too terrifying."

Zero laughed a little. "No, of course not. I'm just glad I was able to see your plan so clearly."

"Well, I couldn't have done it without you."

Zero's visor flashed happily. But Dal took a deep breath and looked down at his hands.

"I wanted to tell you, also—when we were in the cage. Um, I shouldn't have told you to let yourself out of your containment unit, even to get the key." Dal forced himself to look up, over at Zero. "I know—I know what the Diviner did to you was horrible. And I know how horrible you feel about what happened with Gwyn, when she saw your reflection."

Zero put their mechanical hand on Dal's shoulder, quieting him. "We're very lucky that Gwyn wasn't damaged more than she was," they said softly.

"I know," Dal said. "And I know it wasn't your fault. None of us thinks that. But I should never have suggested you do something like that again." He fixed his gaze on the color swirling in Zero's visor—it was all that Dal could ever see of Zero's true form, but it was all he needed to see. "I promise you, from now on, that none of us will ever ask you to remove your containment suit. It'll always be your decision."

Zero was quiet for a long time. Then they nodded. When they spoke, Dal thought he heard a waver in their voice. "Thank you, Dal. That means everything to me."

"It's the least I can do," Dal said.

He stood up, Zero rising alongside him, and walked back to the captain's chair. Gwyn was leaning up against it, watching the viewscreen.

Dal plopped down. "Any ideas where we should go next?"

"No. I like the idea of just—drifting." Gwyn took a deep breath. "Dal, I owe you an apology too."

"What's that? Gwyndala is admitting she was wrong about something?" Dal grinned mischievously at her.

She rolled her eyes. "I owe the whole crew an apology," she said, raising her voice a little. One by one, the others turned back toward her.

"For what?" Rok-Tahk asked, frowning. "You and Murf are the reason we're not still stuck in that cage back on Odaru."

"Yeah, but I shouldn't have left my post," Gwyn said. "It was my job to protect the ship. I mean, it's our home."

Janeway nodded. "I'm at fault here too. I should have been firmer with you about staying on the ship. I'm sorry, everyone."

Dal nodded. "Everyone is forgiven. It all worked out."

"Yeah," Rok-Tahk agreed. "Everything's good as new."

"Well, not exactly." Jankom spun around in his chair. "We still can't fix the transporter."

There was a long pause—then the entire crew dissolved into groans.

The entire crew, except for one person.

"Not so fast," Zero said slyly. "Jankom, I believe you said we needed a phase coil for the transporter, yes?"

Jankom scratched his head. "That is what Jankom Pog said, yeah. But—"

"Will this work?" Zero reached inside their containment unit and removed a slim piece of metal, little lines etched into it.

Jankom gasped. "That's it! How ... ?"

"Well, remember how T'agross opened that crate and took out a phase coil?" Zero said. "I grabbed one as we were making our escape. The crate was still just sitting there, wide open."

Jankom bounded over to Zero, who handed him the phase coil. He flipped it this way and that, frowning a little as he studied it.

"Will it work?" Zero asked nervously.

"It's perfect!" Jankom beamed at Zero. "You've got a good eye. Maybe you could help out in engineering sometime."

"Perhaps," Zero said. They were quiet for a moment, then added, "Although I wish I hadn't had to steal it."

"Oh," Rok-Tahk said brightly. "But you didn't, Zero!" She jumped up from the navigation station, brimming with excitement.

"What do you mean?" Zero asked.

"I just realized it." She grinned, her eyes flashing. "We got the trade we wanted!"

The crew all looked at one another. Even

Janeway, who had been sitting back and observing as the crew hashed out their mission, straightened up a little, her curiosity piqued.

"What do you mean?" Gwyn asked.

"Teyless still has the battery we replicated," she said. "And Zero said they took the phase coil from Teyless's warehouse. So technically, we traded!"

Gwyn and Dal both broke into huge smiles, and Jankom let out a laugh of delight before tossing the phase coil up in the air. It spun, catching the lights of the bridge, then landed back in his hands.

"Well, I suppose that's a relief," Zero said.

"Yeah," Dal said. "Although it wasn't exactly an easy trade, was it?"

"Not *remotely*," Rok-Tahk said with a sigh.

"I would even go so far as to say that attempting to replicate the battery for a trade was far more trouble than it was worth." Zero drifted over alongside Rok-Tahk. "I think Murf agrees with me."

Murf, who was currently attempting to eat the leg of a chair, wiggled a little in response.

"I'm not sure Murf totally understands replication," Gwyn said. "But I agree with you."

"Hey," Dal said. "That replicator saved the day.

That fake chimerium was the only reason we got the traders in the pod."

"Ex-actly," Jankom said.

"Yes," Zero said. "But we wouldn't have needed to trick the traders if we hadn't taken a battery down to the market in the first place."

Jankom frowned, considering this. So did Dal.

"Yeah," Dal said. "Trying to trick a bunch of criminals didn't exactly work out that well for us, did it?" He glanced over his shoulder at Janeway, who had materialized a holographic cup of coffee in one hand. She took a sip, nodding at him.

I'm on the right path, he realized with a start.

"Maybe next time . . . ," he said, scrunching up his shoulders a little. "Maybe we should just use the replicator the way it's supposed to be used."

He braced himself, expecting protests. Instead, the crew nodded their agreement.

"I think that's a good idea," Rok-Tahk said.

"Yeah," Gwyn said. "One of the better ones you've had."

Dal swatted at her in annoyance.

"Yes, we're much better off replicating necessities," Zero added.

Jankom let out a sigh. "It's not as much fun, but in the long term—yeah, Jankom Pog agrees it's better."

Murf burped.

Dal laughed, then turned to the last crew member: Janeway, who took another long sip of her coffee.

"What do you think?" he said, a faint flicker of pride growing in his chest.

Janeway smiled. "I think the Federation would approve of the excellent decision making you've shown here today." She lifted her mug. "All of you."

Dal broke into a huge grin. He turned back to the others, all of them watching him and waiting to hear what he said next.

"Let's see where this ship takes us," he said.

DON'T MISS

SUPERNOVA

ANOTHER ACTION-PACKED NOVEL BASED ON

STAR TREK

PRODIGY™

A NOVEL WRITTEN BY

ROBB PEARLMAN

#1 NEW YORK TIMES *BESTSELLING AUTHOR*

CHAPTER ONE

It was morning on the Federation starship USS *Protostar*. At least, Dal *thought* it was morning. Or, more to the point, he *hoped* it was morning. It was kind of hard to tell what time it was in space without looking at the ship's chronometer. And as helpful as Hologram Janeway was, even Dal recognized how annoying it would be if he'd kept asking her what time it was all sleepless night long.

He'd hardly slept, because every time Dal closed his eyes, he remembered. He remembered how, just a short time ago, he and the rest of the *Protostar*'s crew had been prisoners of the Diviner on Tars Lamora. How the pain from the Watchers' weapons would hurt his body, and how the pain of feeling completely and totally alone, despite being surrounded by hundreds of other Unwanted, would hurt his spirit. Dal tried wrapping himself in his blanket and focusing on the good things that had happened, like finding the Federation starship in which he was now flying through space. How he and his crew joined together to not only escape Tars Lamora, but also to return to that distant planet and liberate the rest of the Unwanted from the Diviner. How happy a little doll created from spare parts could make Gwyn.

But no amount of blanket wrapping could ease his mind. Neither could counting something called sheep or drinking replicated cups of warm milk (both of which, Janeway insisted, were tried-and-true tricks Earthlings used to get to sleep). So every time Dal closed his eyes, he felt like he was immediately transported, hungry, back to the mines of Tars Lamora. Or helpless beneath the cilium tendrils on that M-Class Murder Planet in the Hirogen System that had tried to eat them all. Or stuck in a cage, even just a few days ago in the marketplace on Odaru.

Dal couldn't stop thinking about how they had narrowly escaped with the necessary material to repair the *Protostar*'s transporter system. As much as Dal remembered—and tried to forget—how he'd felt in the past, he also couldn't stop himself from thinking that any amount of hunger or helplessness or fear was worse now because he was not alone. He cared about his crew. Dal was the captain and understood that he had to maintain a brave face for them. If he was brave, they would be brave.

After what seemed like days of just lying there, Dal threw off his blankets, rubbed his eyes, and swung his legs off the side of his bed. "Computer, lights," he said, and his cabin was illuminated in the warm glow of a simulated sunrise. Dal surveyed the room and stepped onto the cold floor, which shocked his bare feet so much, he had to hop around until he found his boots. Starfleet boots were a lot more comfortable than the footwear he had to wear as a prisoner. *Shinier, too,* thought Dal. *Being a captain sure has its perks! And,* he silently admitted, *its responsibilities.*

So it was morning on the USS *Protostar*. Well, it probably was.

And Captain Dal R'El was on duty.

CHAPTER TWO

Dal walked onto the bridge to find Hologram Janeway. Intended as an ETH, an Emergency Training Hologram, to aid and advise the Starfleet-trained personnel that were supposed to be occupying the *Protostar*, this lifelike computer-generated replica of the real Kathryn Janeway was, once again, helping to get a crew back to the safety and security of Starfleet.

Janeway stood, at ease, beside the captain's chair. *Dal's* captain's chair. As much as Dal understood that the *Protostar* was, technically, the property of Starfleet, the ship had quickly become his home, or at least his home away from home—wherever his real home was. And until the ship was returned to Starfleet, Dal had no problem claiming it, and the captain's chair, for himself. And yet, even after all these weeks, Dal still had trouble believing where he was. The sleek lines and temperature-controlled comfort of the *Protostar*'s bridge were a far cry from the rough-hewn, broiling-hot mines of Tars Lamora. The gleaming utilitarian silver and gray of the circular bridge were warmed by the view seen through the massive bank of almost-floor-to-ceiling windows lining its front third.

"Good morning, Dal," said Janeway.

"Morning, Janeway," said Dal, sliding into the seat. *His* seat.

"Morning?" asked Janeway.

"It is morning, isn't it?" Dal searched the bridge for the closest chronometer. Janeway lifted her hologram mug of coffee to her lips and smiled. "Oh, it *is* morning, Dal," she said, pausing to sip, "but from the looks of you, I'd agree it's probably not a good one for you. At all."

"Ohhh. Do I look that bad?" asked Dal, leaning toward his boot to inspect his own purple reflection in its shine. Janeway herself never looked anything but pristine and Starfleet-manual ready. Her official uniform, a black jumpsuit with maroon shoulders, fit perfectly over her gray shirt. The shine of her gold combadge paled only in comparison to her wit and intellect. Dal's confidence in himself was matched only by his respect for his holographic adviser. As captain of the *Protostar*, Dal's was the final word. But that didn't mean that he couldn't take her suggestions and ideas under advisement.

Janeway leaned in. "I wouldn't say you look bad, Dal, but you do have more rings beneath your eyes than Saturn has around its middle. Did you get any sleep at all? Did you record your captain's log yet?"

Dal turned and, in a clumsy effort to change the subject, busied himself by pushing some colorful spots on the console embedded in the arm of the chair. "I got enough. Don't worry about me! I'm just fine. Looking good and captaining like any captain would captain! I'll do the log later. It's too early to log." Dal wondered if the *Protostar*'s life-support systems kept track of his resting and waking hours. Could it tell when he was sleeping? Could it monitor things like respiration or heartbeats? Would Janeway call his bluff and check?

"You're the captain," said Janeway.

Phew, thought Dal as he alternated between reading the same flashing notices on his personal operations station and trying to tame the gray and white hair that stuck up in all directions from the top of his head. Somewhere between decks, the lights in a Jefferies Tube were flashing on and off. From the controls on the captain's chair, Dal tried to fix the issue. Janeway's programming allowed for Starfleet personnel, especially those still learning, to test and find their own limits. She was confident, based on the crew's performance thus far, that they would continue to grow, even if part of that growth was learning how to fail. But, just in case, she ran a diagnostic to make sure the lights in the tube were on when Dal was finished messing around.

The doors at the back of the bridge swooshed open as Jankom Pog, the ship's engineer, walked in.

"Jankom Pog loves breakfast food," he said. "If only I could have breakfast food all day long. Wait—could I? Did Jankom Pog just invent a new thing?"

Zero floated in behind him. "I do not think so, Jankom," they said, taking their place at the helm.

"Whadda you know about eating, Zero?" asked Jankom, stuffing the last replicated Delvan fluff pastry into his mouth. "You're noncorporeal—you have no mouth to eat with!"

"That is true," Zero agreed, tapping the area on their metal containment suit where their mouth would be, "but that doesn't mean I haven't heard of the ancient Earth tradition sometimes described by the acronym 'ADB.'"

"'ADB'?" asked Dal. "What's 'ADB'?"

"Ac-ro-nym? What's an acronym?" asked Jankom.

"An acronym is an abbreviation of an idea or concept, using the first letters of each word in a phrase. In this case, 'ADB' stands for All-Day Breakfast. During ADB, families and friends gather for lunch or dinner, but prepare and consume food that would normally be served during the morning repast."

Jankom was astounded. "Is that … can it be true, Janeway?"

"It is, but I usually keep to just coffee in the morning," she said, taking yet another sip of her seemingly bottomless mug. "And in the evening."

"I meant, is that what 'acronym' means?" clarified Jankom. "But Jankom is glad to have all the information so he can ask for ADB at any time of day. Or night!"

Once again, the doors to the bridge swooshed

open, revealing the rest of the *Protostar*'s crew—Gwyn, Rok-Tahk, and Murf.

"Brrrrrblpthhhhlslllll," greeted Murf.

"I think Murf means 'Good morning,'" said Rok-Tahk merrily, "but he did say the same thing when I accidentally stepped on him yesterday, so who knows."

"Jankom made that sound after too much gagh once," said Jankom, spinning around in his chair. The rest of the crew decided to not ask questions.

"Ooookay," Rok-Tahk said, trying to move the conversation along. "Where are we off to today?"

Dal straightened in his seat. "I think we'll still go, um . . . that way," he said, pointing directly ahead.

"Oh, so the way we've been going?" asked Rok-Tahk.

"Yep. That's the way to Starfleet, so that's the way we'll go!" Dal replied confidently.

"Brrrrrblpthhhhlslllll," said Murf. Again.

Gwyn stood silently beside Zero at their navigation station and stared thoughtfully out the windows that took up the bow of the *Protostar*'s bridge. She traced the gold fretwork on her arm. It looked like an intricate piece of jewelry, but this fretwork was not mere decoration. It was a Vau N'Akat heirloom given to her by her father. She could control it with her mind and shape it into any configuration. Gwyn often absentmindedly touched her heirloom when she was deep in thought.

Gwyn was not, and would probably never be, known as "a morning person." She awoke each day not with Rok-Tahk's boundless optimism, or even Jankom's insatiable hunger, but with the lingering, biting memories of mornings on Tars Lamora. It was in those early hours, sometimes even before she had a chance to wipe the sleep from her eyes, when Drednok, her father's attendant, would give her a list of orders for the day. Her entire day would be laid out for her. Days filled with trading bars of chimerium with Kazon for new Unwanted. Days spent spying on miners, translating, squashing uprisings, and figuring out ways to manage some sort of independence with Drednok's glowing red eyes constantly watching her. All the while wondering what her father's ultimate plan was, and whether she was right to help him. Gwyn's father was known to her and to everyone on Tars Lamora as the Diviner. She was his progeny, and he was ruthless in trying to train her to fight. And how to kneel. Drednok sensed that Gwyn questioned her father's motives, and made it very clear to her, whenever he could, that she would be wise to not overstep her boundaries. He made his distrust of Gwyn known to the Diviner.

It was difficult to make out a lot of details of the stars and planets that whizzed by at warp speed, but she was able to discern enough to know that the crew was hurtling through space at what would have been an unthought-of velocity just a few weeks ago. And some of the twinkling stars reminded her of the shimmers she saw in the eyes of the last Unwanted she bartered for. A young Caitian female whose eyes, like those of most of the young prisoners forced to work in the mines beneath the planet's surface, would probably never sparkle in the sun again. She was proud of herself and the rest of the crew that they had recently returned to Tars Lamora to free the Unwanted, but Gwyn had spent far too many mornings in dread to ever say, let alone think, *Good morning*.

Gwyn had so desperately wanted to see the stars for so long that she was rarely able to turn away from them these days. And now here, on the bridge of the *Protostar*, far away from the yoke of the Diviner and Drednok, and surrounded by the safety and support of a crew—of friends—she was able to just . . . look at them. She found herself absentmindedly stroking the nest of fine, dead filament that made up the hair of the doll she'd picked up in the marketplace on Odaru. Since that adventure, Gwyn had kept the doll close to her at all times. She looked at it, a hodgepodge of old starship parts clothed in a dress made of silk scraps, and thought of that young Caitian. Had she ever had a doll like this? Had any of the Unwanted? Gwyn could not recall.

Gwyn raised the doll to her own face. It cast a shadow as they flew by a bright star, surely serving as a sun around which a planet or planets orbited. Its light, and the light of her friends and crewmates, warmed her more than the sun above Tars Lamora ever had.

"Gwyn," said Zero, shaking her out of her fog of memory. "There is something engraved on the foot of your doll."

CASSANDRA ROSE CLARKE is the author of *Our Lady of the Ice, Magic of Blood and Sea, Magic of Wind and Mist, Star's End, Halo: Battle Born*, and *Halo: Meridian Divide*. She grew up in south Texas and currently lives in Richmond, Virginia, where she tends to multiple cats. Cassandra's first adult novel, *The Mad Scientist's Daughter*, was a finalist for the 2013 Philip K. Dick Award, and her YA novel, *The Assassin's Curse*, was nominated for YALSA's 2014 Best Fiction for Young Adults. Her short fiction has appeared in *Strange Horizons* and *Daily Science Fiction*. Visit her at CassandraRoseClarke.com.